The Colour *Of* Rain

Cover Of Rain

Alex Skalding

Wynkin deWorde

2002

Published in 2002
by

Wynkin deWorde

Wynkin deWorde
PO Box 257, Tuam Road, Galway, Ireland
Copyright © Alex Skalding, 2002
All rights reserved

A CIP catalogue record for this book is available from the British Library

ISBN: 0-9542607-2-4

Typeset by Patricia Hope, Skerries, Co. Dublin, Ireland
Cover Illustration by Jimmy Lawlor
Illustrations by Roger Derham
Design by Design Direct, Galway, Ireland
Printed by BETAPRINT, Dublin, Ireland.

J126,551
£14.00

Thank Yous

This book is dedicated to all children with adventure on their minds and to all parents minding those adventures.

I want to thank in particular, in alphabetical order, Jeff Hanley, Sinead Lalor, Mille Mantle, Deirdre and Gráinne McCarthy, for taking the time to tell me what colour means to them and for reading and advising me on the early drafts.

To my own children, adults now, and the memory of bedtime stories long ago.

To Valerie Shortland, my editor, for her great help and guidance.

THE STORYTELLER

⁂〰ᛗ ♦♦□□⬜♦ᛗ●●ᛗ□

When I was smaller nobody ever explained to me what people really meant when they talked about *'stuff'*; everybody used the word but then they all seemed to mean a different thing when they used it.

I had to find out for myself about what *'stuff'* meant and along the way sometimes had to find out the hard way, but then I guess, all of us do like.

For me right now, *'stuff'* is everything that happens, everything that I like and hate, the good and the bad, the hard and the soft, the weird and the not so weird. It can make you sad or happy, angry or nice and cold or warm. Knowing *'stuff'* is how I learn about the world I live in, the type of people I meet, the places that I go, but most importantly, it's how I learn about myself.

Sometimes *'stuff'* happens and it's easy to understand and explain because it directly concerns you; something like your first kiss or the first real big fright you ever got.

In my case, they were one and the same thing and I'd better tell you about it before we go any further so you can have some idea of what I'm like. It's not that I'm shy or anything, it's just that when it comes to girls I am fierce slow and at one point they, the other lads like, got worried about my 'psycho' and said that

1

this fear was something they needed to sort out for me. '*Stuckonmyownwithagirlphobia*', they called it.

Having set it all up behind my back, with Suzy 'Tulips' O'Farrell, as a dare, they all said her kisses were to die for and I should go for it.

"At you Bull!" they shouted at me as I headed for the woods.

"Right back at you, lads," I shouted back, trying not to look as nervous as I felt.

I have to tell you that spiders, maggots or dark places never bothered me much but the thought of being stuck on my own with a girl, who wanted do things to me like, really scared the colour out of me. There we were, Suzy 'Tulips' O'Farrell and myself deep in the woods, together like. When it came to the time for the kiss, I tried to duck. Too late! Suzy was faster than she looked and latched onto me like the plunger my dad uses to clear blocked drains and sinks. She wouldn't let go. I then knew what the lads meant by dying from one of her kisses. I nearly did from a lack of air!

It was a little while before I copped on to what the problem was. Suzy couldn't let go! We both had braces in our teeth at the time and it was the worse case of 'locktooth' syndrome he had ever seen, the Doc said. The hospital had to separate us, with a wire-clippers, while Suzy's mother kept threatening me with the police and saying that I would have to pay for new braces for her daughter.

Frightening stuff, man!

On a more serious note, as adults would say when they want to stop each other having fun, sometimes '*stuff*' happens which is impossible to explain and understand fully, but it just happens and we're cool about it, like. When my grandpa died, and I had to watch him being put into the grave, nobody really could explain to me why someone who was really so nice goes and dies on you. I was fierce upset at the time like, but got over it eventually.

Sometimes however, really weird '*stuff*' happens to other people that must be talked about because, even if you don't think it concerns or affects you, it actually does and you need to know about it. Knowledge is everything because, as my granny likes to spout, and perhaps she's right ignorance is not bliss, it's just ignorance.

Ignorance, or the act of ignoring *'stuff'* can also be dangerous and trying to prevent some of that danger is the main reason for the story you are about to read.

Some really weird *'stuff'* happened to a gang of seven boys and girls, including me, whom you don't know, but what happened to us changed everything for everybody. Now we weren't a gang that normally hung out together, in fact some of us didn't like each other that much, but in the end that didn't matter. We were thrown together and had to get on with it like. You need to know about what happened to us and they, the other dudes in the gang, wanted me to tell you the story.

My name is Fintan Sheehan, but the lads call me Bull because round where I live I'm known as the storyteller. Now I'm not one of those famous storytelling writers you hear about who disappear off to Paris, and spend all their time drinking, smoking and getting married. How I wish like. No, the furthest I've ever gone under my own steam was cycling to Banteer and even then I got a puncture. I've sort of got sandy hair with freckles on my face and skin that peels off in layers when the sun hits it. I'm what you would call a little bit fat, or what my granny calls 'generous' but it has its advantages in that I'm a pretty good goalkeeper.

Now, I've always wanted to write a book like, and had even designed the cover in my head. It was going to have a big picture of me smiling out at you and was going to have a health warning stamped on the side in big red letters, like those written on the side of cigarette packets. The stamp would say something like 'Reading can damage your wealth', or 'Reading when preggers causes small babies', or 'Reading when driving causes death', or even 'Kissing Tulips is fatal' and I'd crack myself up thinking of even more disgusting ones.

Unfortunately, things don't always work out the way you want.

This book is not all a laugh and I had to go a bit easy on the wisecracks. What I mean to say is, that the '*stuff*' that happened us, the '*stuff*' I'm meant to write about, was really, really weird.

Even to this day I can't pretend to understand everything that went down. Its not that I'm thick like, but when so much '*stuff*' happens to you all at once it sometimes gets very confusing. I've written down nearly everything that I can remember and perhaps you'll have better luck figuring it all out.

In fact, I know you will, but take great care! Although I haven't stamped one on the cover, this book *does* come with a health warning, which is, '*Reading can annoy weasels*'. If I might give you one small bit of advice like, it's this: look behind you and around you before you start to read. Indeed, if you can manage it, read with only one eye because that will free up the other one to keep watch.

There are dark, dark forces and ugly, evil things all around us that don't want this story to be told or read, so, if by chance you happen to meet a weasel while reading it, spit him in the eye for all of us because **F** is riding on his back.

1

THE RAIN

❄︎〰︎♏︎ ☼♋︎♓︎■

Some of you won't remember the time but I swear on my last page of dry paper, and I'm not lying either, it **Rain**ed and **Rain**ed and **Rain**ed and **Rain**ed. (Please remember if you are going to swear on something, it must be done on something really precious to you; something that you would not like to lose.)

It **rain**ed so much, and for so long, that people forgot what it was like to be dry and even forgot some of the words we once used to describe the dry time. People stopped counting the hours and instead called them the *'showers'*, days were *'sprays'*, weeks were *'leaks'*, and years were *'tears'*. Months were called *'lunths'*, because some eejit couldn't find another word to rhyme with month so he invented one. This was made up of the first three letters of the word, 'lunar' meaning the moon, and the last three letters of 'baths', which we used to have to take once a lunth but didn't bother any more because of all the rain.

It was **wet**, **wet**ter than wet, the **wettest** wet yet. Each tear was made up of twelve lunths, and was given a name, like the Chinese do. The first tear of the rain was the Tear of the Bucket, and last tear was the Tear of the Cats and Dogs.

Everywhere was **damp**, **damp**er than **damp**, and the **damp**est dumped-on place of all was my hometown of Dripsey, in the

County of Cork, Ireland. My mum, dad and granny complained and complained, but it still rained.

Drip, drip, drip, drip, drip! It was enough to do your head in like, but there was some craic to be had all the same!

Getting ready in the morning to go to school was a real laugh, like. Cross my heart, we had to dress like deep-sea divers and cover ourselves from head to foot in a rubber wet suit. Everybody had a wet suit after the government decided to give one to every school-kid in the country, even the hill-billys.

Sadly, of course, there were some lucky people like Sheevra Devine, who got really special wet suits because they said they had allergies. Her mum was related to somebody really important in the government. I've an allergy to Sheevra Devine like, but I didn't get a special one.

These lucky sickos got wet suits, which were bright yellow with orange collars and red zips and what's more, they didn't even smell like the black rubber ones the rest of us had to wear. Everybody I know hated the smell of wet rubber and lots tried saying that they also had allergies.

The Devine's relative in the Government's Department of the Changing Environment (DOCE for short.) came on the television and said that only people with previously known ante-diluvian allergies (AnDAs) could apply for the special wet suits. They were already swamped with requests, he said, and would not be able to meet the demand until next tear.

We're all friggin' swamped, I thought, and what the hell was ante-diluvian anyway.

Mister Penhaligan, our teacher, said it meant 'before the Flood'; Noah's one like.

We sometimes went to school on a raft of beer barrels that Kegs Murphy's dad had made. We called him Kegs' dad but according to Kegs, he wasn't really. Kegs said he was adopted. Where did Mister Murphy get all the barrels? I wondered. He didn't even have a pub. You never saw Kegs' adopted dad out and about much. 'It took time to get the barrels ready for raft making,' Kegs said. 'They had to be really, really empty, like, and that took a lot of work,' he said. Yeah right! Whenever Tricks and I sneaked, well barrel-rolled really, over to the Murphy house all we could hear was snoring coming from the back bedroom. Well, that and the sound of the television, which he always left on.

THE RAIN TIME

James 'Tricks' Kirby, he was called that because he was full of them, came into the classroom one spray with a snorkel attached to his wet suit. Everybody laughed because they thought he was messing, but Tricks wasn't.

He was worried like, really worried about all the rain, he said. His dad's farm was by now, under one and a bit metres of water, and it was still rising, the Department of the Changing Environment (DOCE) had warned. Tricks said he was sweating because he was only just 1m 40cm tall.

The snorkel was really important to him and he cried when Mister Penhaligan took it away. Tricks Kirby had never cried before. In fact he was the bravest person I knew. Once he even slept, well stayed, in the graveyard for a whole night like.

On Sky and Sea satellite television news they showed how a lake had formed in the Sahara and how a mad Frenchman was trying to windsurf from Cairo to Timbuktu. The lady reporter talking to him, Katie Allteeth, made a joke about ships of the desert but the Frenchman didn't laugh. In fact he looked very serious. He was dead right, I thought, it was a really stupid joke like.

I told Mickey 'Atlas' Malone, my very, very best friend that particular leak, and whose wet suit was full of patches, that I'd love to go to Timbuktu, except I didn't know where it was. He showed it to me on the map of the world in the school.

"Look, head." (Atlas called everybody 'head'!) He said, pointing to a small dry spot on the map, "There it is. The right spelling is Tombouctou and it's in Mali, on the edge of the Sahara desert."

"How come you knew that like?" I asked.

"I need to know where I am, even if I'm not there, head." He answered.

Besides being wicked deep, Mickey Malone knew everything about that map, and that's why we called him Atlas like. After he left to do some more deep stuff of his own, I stared at the map for a long time.

The dry spot where Timbuktu was on the map, was very, very strange, I thought, like weird almost. The rest of the map and the wall behind it were wet through.

Sky and Sea News also showed where a family called the van Winkles in Holland were all electrocuted when they fell asleep in front of their televisions and the water from a burst dyke rushed into the house and covered the plugs. Atlas said that if they had been wearing rubber shoes and a wet suit nothing would have happened to them.

Except be killed by the smell eventually, I thought. I also wondered for a moment whether Sheevra Devine's special AnDA suit would protect her from electrocution as she had cut the feet off so's she could wear her new high-heeled wellies.

All of the leaders and the people who thought themselves to be really important from around the world, including the Devine's relative from the Department of the Changing Environment – by now we were calling him IL DOCE – met on a English ship called the Ark Royal, to talk about the rain and what they could do about it. They also argued about the AnDA's problem and the sudden and huge demand, 'deluge' they called it, for special wet suits. Eventually, they all promised to get their factories to increase the production of the special yellow and orange wet suits, with red zips, to help solve the problem. They needed to get off their backsides as well, like.

Waiting, with Katie Allteeth and thousands of other reporters, back in the port for the Ark Royal to dock after the conference, was a medicine man called Chief Crazy Watercourse. He was from a Native-American-Indian-reservation retirement home, called the Four Directions, in New Mexico and was filmed doing the raindance backwards. He was also shown throwing burning cedar sticks up into the air and shouting up at the sky 'Be quiet, o breath of twins'. (Apparently some Indians blame twins for everything and the Noggin twins in our class were very annoyed about this.)

It didn't do much good like. The Great Mystery – that's what he called God – wasn't listening. All the fired-up cedar sticks soon fizzled out and Crazy Watercourse looked miserable and sad. The feathers in his big headdress were soaked and they sagged terribly. The war-paint on his face ran down his cheeks and chest like dirty great tears.

Cissy Hourihan, whose dad was the local vet, and who kept pet snakes in her bedroom, said he wasn't doing it properly and shouldn't have been let out of the reservation retirement home. Cissy knew all about things like that. The Noggin twins thought she was a bit of witch like, into Wicca and vampire-slaying and stuff. Tricks didn't like her much either as he thought she was the sneaky but secret gang-leader of the school bullies who annoyed him when he first went.

Talking of weirdoes, a voodoo half-Indian witchdoctor from Haiti (Atlas Malone showed me where this was on the map.) promised that he could stop the rain if only he could get his magic stick back. There was little chance of that, it appeared, as he had swapped his stick for a special yellow and orange wet suit, with red zips, from a Japanese voodoo-stick collector who had now disappeared into the Brazilian jungle.

An Amazonian Indian from the same jungle blamed the cutting down of the rainforest for the rain.

An Indian woodcutter – when he could find wood to cut – from Bangalore, blamed America for all its oil-burning pollution and tried spitting the ashes from a fire back at the sky while singing 'Water is the Sakravi' song, again and again. You probably don't know but this song was a number one hit in the Sea-Saw Charts during the Tear of the Bucket.

Finally, a big-eyed, head-shaking, red-turban-wearing Indian weatherman – his name was Kneedeep Inrainov Singh –, working for the Russian space agency in Siberia, blamed a meteor shower.

They were all playing cowboys and Indians in the end. Nobody in the government's Department of Indian Affairs (DOIA) or amongst the People who Thought Themselves Really

Important (PeTTRIs) had a clue what to do about the rain but, they sure knew how to try and look around for someone or something to blame. They could sure dish it out like!

It reminded me of the scene at home when something unusual happened, like once when a blackberry-scuttering bird (I mean of course a bird who had eaten lots of blackberries and whose droppings are then purple) came down the chimney. The bird, as frightened as we were surprised, left a trail of purple crap across the room when trying to escape. Us kids, and me in particular, were blamed, as if we had invited the stupid bird to drop down the chimney in the first place.

Where would all this blaming end? I wondered for a while before my worst fears were realised and somebody threatened to start a war.

They showed on the Sky and Sea News that a gathering of all the desert tribes of Arabia had suddenly declared war on Nepal – where Mount Everest, the highest mountain in the world, is to be found – and were making plans for Operation Oasis, as they called it.

"Why on earth would you do that? What had the people of Nepal ever done to the tribes in Arabia?" asked the reporter, Katie Allteeth sweetly.

"Nothing really . . ." an Arab sheik, dressed in a beautiful white anti-allergy wet suit with a gold snorkel attached, replied, ". . . but the people in Nepal have very high mountains and we don't. It's the will of Allah, the will of God!"

Miss Allteeth thought this to be a very reasonable answer. The Nepalese people could then blame God for the rain, she said, and their troubles with the Arabians.

Sheevra Devine was really jealous of the sheik's chic wet suit and she blamed IL DOCE for not getting her one.

It wasn't long before everybody else in the world agreed that God or the Great Mystery was to blame.

The time for the war drew closer and closer. Everybody was

taking sides. Nobody was listening. People felt frightened in their wet suits and were even afraid to take them off to go to the toilet.

We were all browned off and the smell got worse and worse like.

2

THE LOSS OF COLOUR

❄︎〰︎♏︎ ☺︎◻︎•• ◻︎↗ ✋︎◻︎●◻︎◆◻︎

Suddenly, one morning at ten hundred showers (We'd all begun to speak like sailors.), on the twenty-fourth spray, in the last leak, of the tenth lunth, in the Tear of the Cats and Dogs, it stopped raining.

Just stopped like!

No more drips in Dripsey or anywhere else for that matter. People were dancing for joy in places as far apart as Wellington, in New Zealand, Bootle, in England and Dryanova, in Bulgaria. Mister Murphy's boat of beer barrels, Norah's Flotation Device, – he had named it after Norah O'Toole, the barmaid in his favourite pub – was not needed.

Tricks Kirby never had to use his snorkel – in any event he had grown nearly 3cm since the rains began – and we were all able to take off the wet suits. All the countries of the world declared a Smelly-Rubber-Wet Suit Freedom day. The singer Drybono and the band Uboat-2 gave a free concert to help poorer countries get out of their depth problems. People were friends again.

They smelt better at any rate!

The Arabian chic sheiks pulled back from going to war with Nepal and the Japanese voodoo-stick collector came out from the jungle. The Frenchman nearly made it to Timbuktu on his windsurfer.

'One more lunth of rain would have been enough,' he said on the news.

The French government said he had too much water on his brain, that his family were all madmen, that his family had always been madmen, and that he should be locked up for wishing for more rain. Even Chief Crazy Watercourse was interviewed on his way home to the reservation retirement home – still walking backwards – about the windsurfer's wishes and he also agreed with the French government. All the PeTTRIs did.

The strange thing was like, that the dry spot where Timbuktu was on our school's map, had never ever got damp. Cissy Hourihan couldn't explain it and we had just about given up trying to, when Jambo piped up from the very back of the classroom.

"Wa . . . wa . . . wa . . . one moment, fif . . . fif . . . if you please," he stuttered in a very deep voice.

Jambo Kitangiri stood up and walked to stand in front of the map. He said nothing for a while but then, in the same deep voice, informed us that many African peoples had powerful secrets and that the people of Timbuktu must be the most powerful of all. We just let him get on with it like.

Jambo was a strange kid, nice, but really strange. And it wasn't because he was black and came from Africa, no man; he would have been different whatever colour he was. He had a stutter when he talked but when he sang he didn't. So whenever he had to say a lot, he didn't, but sang it instead. On top of all that, he had an enormous backside.

When he came to the school first, we asked him his name and he just said, 'He . . . he . . . hello'; when we asked him where he was from, he said, 'He . . . he . . . hello,' and when we asked him what age he was, he again said, 'He . . . he . . . hello.'

His real name was actually Samuel but when his dad, Mister Kitangiri, came to the school and explained that 'hello' was the only English word Samuel knew, we decided to call him Jambo, which Mister Penhaligan said was 'hello' in Swahili. It was Jambo that noticed when all the hassle began.

Now you'd think that with all the rain we had enough trouble but that was just the start of it.

One spray, a lunth or so after the rains had stopped, Jambo came running up to the hideout that we used for our secret den. We were busy getting rid of the sandbags and some of the barrels belonging to Norah's Floatation Device.

"Jambo, Jambo!" Tricks called out.

"How's it going, head?" Atlas added.

"Not good. I am de . . . de . . . deeply concerned, my friends." Jambo looked serious.

"Why?" we asked. "What's up, Jambo?"

"I've just come from my dw . . . dw . . . dwelling." Jambo stopped what he was saying and started singing instead. "My family were watching the television and suddenly noticed that the mad Frenchman's bright red sail was no longer red. They communicated this puzzlement with our neighbours and they informed us it was the same in their dwellings."

Let me say at this point, in case there is any confusion, the people of Dripsey generally live in houses. Jambo however, insists on calling them dwellings, saying that where he was from it had something to do with living close to a source of water.

He went on to tell us that people all over the town were checking their televisions and trying to tune them in again. First they would let the set do it automatically but when that didn't work they were spending hours pressing the remote controls before finally giving up and shouting at the sets in disgust.

We all belted home to see this outbreak of television abuse

and as we passed by the back of Kegs Murphy's house we could hear his adopted dad inside, shouting at the television in his bedroom. The curtains were closed so we couldn't see anything but the poor television was getting some severe abuse like. In addition to the thumping and crashing sounds, Mister Murphy was roaring out, 'Flaming Norah. Oh, flaming Norah. Oh, flaming Norrrrrrah!', time and time again.

He didn't sound like an unhappy beer barrel to me like, and so we hung around for a while to see if we could spot what was happening. Kegs wasn't there at the time and perhaps it was just as well he had gone shopping with Missus Murphy in the city. He was very attached to the television.

Soon all the noise stopped and it went deadly quiet in the Murphy house. We could then hear Mister Murphy's snoring starting and were just about to leave when we suddenly spotted Norah O'Toole sneaking out the back door. It was too good an opportunity to let go.

Hiding behind some empty barrels, Tricks and I shouted out "Flaming Norah!" at the top of our voices before running away. She screamed. Mister Murphy came flaking out after us from the house but he wasn't fast enough like. He was cursing like mad and had a very high colour. Even from a long way away I could still see that.

Tricks said he supposed that Norah O'Toole was probably good with televisions.

"Yeah right, head!" Atlas laughed.

Mister Murphy would do anything to get some colour back in his life, I thought.

I was puffing like mad from the chase when I got home. There was pandemonium inside the living room. The rest of the family were hovering around the television set and saying that every programme was like all the old cowboy and Charlie Chaplin movies. No matter what was done to adjust the television the pictures remained in black and white.

I didn't notice any difference, and I said so like.

"Spoofer!" my big brother, Seamus, shouted as he gave me an almighty thump.

"Liar, liar, pants on fire!" my five-year-old sister, Tara shouted.

They would have been if Mister Murphy had caught us! I thought.

My own dad didn't mind, he said, he liked all the old stuff anyway. God he's so ancient like. You know what I mean? He's never understood what Homer Simpson was really on about.

The television stations said it wasn't their fault. The Department of the Changing Environment said it wasn't their fault either.

Soon other stuff began to happen.

To her horror, and my delight, Sheevra Devine's mother complained that her precious daughter's beautiful special wet suit was no longer yellow with orange collars and red zips. Sheevra Devine had refused to take the suit off when the rain stopped, so it served her right.

People all over Dripsey were rushing to 'Four Your Eyes Only', the eye testing shop run by Sheevra Devine's father, an optician.

They complained that all the umbrellas, which were finally being taken down after the rain, had lost their colour. To them the sky was now grey, the trees and the grass were shades of black and grey and when animals, people, and machinery moved, they just looked like shadows creeping in a dark forest.

The Sky and Sea television news said that people all over the world were experiencing the same problem. Katie Allteeth reported that the colour in the world was fading away and that people were frightened.

IL DOCE and the PeTTRIs were even more confused than usual.

It was being called the Shadow Time.

Strange thing though! I wasn't frightened at all like. I could still see everything in colour but nobody would believe me. I told Atlas and he said he was the same. Tricks Kirby also said he could still see in colour but when he had insisted on this to the relief teacher, Miss Busteed – Mister Penhaligan had suddenly gone home on urgent family business to Cornwall – she had threatened to smack poor Tricks with his confiscated snorkel.

None of our families would believe us even though we were blue in the face telling them.

Other people in the town soon began to look at Atlas, Tricks and me very strangely. There was an old woman in our local shop who wanted to cut off a piece of my hair. Atlas Malone nearly lost his trousers and his 'head'. Tricks Kirby however was happy out. He started signing autographs for some of the girls in the secondary school.

Imagine it: all of those really big girls wanting to be with the three of us! It was wicked like. We were like pop-idols.

A little later however, a lot of weirdo strangers and television reporters, including Katie Allteeth, started coming to the town asking about us. There were rumours flying about that we would be taken away to a secret research cave in the mountains.

We all became frightened and after a few leaks of this harassment the three of us sat down in the hideout and decided to form a pact. We'd tell everybody that we'd just been messing, and that all along we were seeing things in black and white just like them.

So, to be like all the rest, we stopped using colour words except black, white and grey. We had to be very careful though.

II. DOCE AND KATIE ALLTEETH

People still watched us suspiciously, wondering whether we were telling the truth or not. When they got angry, and in Mister Murphy's case it was every time he saw me, we could still see the red flush on their faces but never said. When people wore outfits of purple, green and yellow we didn't laugh even though they were a bit like dummies in a fancy-dress parade. Even at home when my Mum got dressed in the morning she would ask my eldest sister, Jane how the shading suited her.

"Very grey-scaled," she would answer approvingly in a posh big-city accent.

Jane used be a painter but she had made a career switch to shadowing instead. Shadowing had become very big business. I wanted to scream that the colours were horrible but they seemed to have forgotten what colour meant and so I said nothing.

The worst of all like, was that the big girls from the secondary school began to ignore us again, calling us stupid

19

kids like. Tricks wanted to tell them, just them mind you, that he could still see colours. Atlas and I had to tie him to what remained of Norah's Flotation Device until he saw sense.

Flaming Norah! Things got worse! Much worse like.

That winter the world got colder. Showers – hours in the old, Before-Rain Language – were now called 'cowers', sprays were now 'greys', leaks were now 'bleaks' and tears were now 'fears'. The Tear of the Cat and Dog ended and it was followed by the Fear of the Black Ice.

The French windsurfer said he was now going to try and skate from Cairo to Timbuktu. Frost and snow covered the ground and stayed there. Spring didn't come. There was a constant cold, grey fog and the adults said it was hard to even see the shadows move. Because of all the rain in the previous two fears nothing had grown except some rice, and this remained frozen in the ice. (Sorry about that crappy rhyme. It slipped in like!)

It was slip, **slip**, **slip** in **slipsy** Dripsey.

Animals, even when they managed to find some food, couldn't tell a rotten plant from a good one and began to die off from, what Cissy Hourihan's dad, the vet, said was colour-blind poisoning or BoCoBSE to give it its right name.

"What does BoCoBSE mean?" we asked Cissy.

"Bovine Colour Blind Scurvy Elephantitis," she said as if we should already know that. Cows and elephants were the worst affected, she said, because they had no more vitamin C.

I suggested collecting the crap from scuttering blackberry-eating birds and giving it to the cows. Nobody listened to what I thought was a brilliant idea like.

For people it got even worse. A special – meaning really cheap – medicine, which the Government had developed to treat all the people with AnDAs allergies, instead of giving them the more expensive special wet suits, suddenly began attacking people's insides.

It made them sick, sicker than sick, smelly **sick** everywhere. It was called the PANDA virus, the black-and-white-Puking-Ante-Diluvian-Allergy virus. Yuk! Even to me it looked like black and white lumps of snot.

Everybody – the Governments, the PeTTRIs and even IL DOCE in the Department of the Changing Environment was really worried like.

One grey, Mister Penhaligan got us all together in our classroom and told us the school would have to close because of the PANDA virus. He looked like he was nearly crying. Some of the girls were too, those who weren't getting sick in the toilet like. Sheevra Devine seemed to be ok, however, which was unusual, as she used spend ages most mornings getting sick in the toilet; could never keep her breakfast down, it seemed.

In case he changed his mind we all got up and started to rush out.

"One moment you lot," his voice boomed out. We all stopped in our tracks. "Fintan Sheehan (Bull to you!), Samuel Kitangiri, Mickey Malone, Kegs Murphy – everybody, including Mister Penhaligan, had forgotten what Kegs real first name was – James Kirby, Cissy Hourihan and Sheevra Devine please stay behind. I want to talk to you."

We sat there while all the others went off home. The Noggin twins made faces at us in the window before running away. I saw that Suzy 'Tulips' O'Farrell was with them. I just hoped they knew what they were letting themselves in for.

The rest of us, those of us who had to stay behind, were dead nervous like, and even a bit worried. None of us knew what we'd done wrong. Anyway, I thought, goody too-high-heeled-wellingtons Sheevra Devine – still in her yellow and orange, sorry, grey wet suit – was asked to stay behind as well.

J/26, 551

3

PUFFER PENHALIGAN

ᚹᚢᚾᚾᛖᚱ ᚹᛖᚾᚺᚨᛚᛁᚷᚨᚾ

We waited there for ages like, saying nothing and wondering what was up. Mister Penhaligan had gone out to his office. I thought I could hear him talking to someone.

Suddenly the door opened and Mister Penhaligan walked back in. Our mouths dropped. Behind him was a weird, and I mean really weird, old geezer. He was very, very tall, had long silver-grey hair tied in a ponytail by an orange ribbon and pulled back through the spout-hole of a knitted, blue-wool tea-cosy that sat on his head. He had an equally long beard that seemed to hold up his short-legged trousers. He had an enormous forehead and big, drooping eyes, which looked even bigger as he stared at us through thick, red-rimmed glasses that sat – just about! – on the end of his nose. He had a baggy yellow suit on, over a green shirt, and had socks of a deep-blue and purple.

"Indigo and violet, young man, not deep-blue and purple," he said suddenly.

Flaming Norah, I thought. He was staring at me and must have known what I was thinking. If that was the case then he must also have known that I could see in colour. He was the first adult I had heard use colour words in ages, even if I didn't know what the colours indigo and violet were really like. What's wrong with deep-blue and purple anyway? I thought.

Puffer Penhaligan's Wrinkles

"They are not colours of the rainbow, are they Miss Hourihan?"

Cissy Hourihan nearly fell off her chair. She mumbled a quick no, and he smiled. His mouth was full of gold-capped teeth that sparkled.

"Children, this is Sir Raphael Bombast Penhaligan, my Uncle. He wants to talk to you," Mister Penhaligan said quietly.

Why us? I thought. Pick on some other gombeens like.

"Because, Mister Sheehan," he was looking at me again. (I promised myself to stop thinking.) "All of you are the only people left in the world who can still see in colour and unless we get moving, you too will soon lose that gift."

All of us? Did he mean Jambo, Cissy, Kegs and Sheevra Devine, of all people, could also see in colour. Atlas and Tricks winked at me. Wicked!

Nobody said anything for a while, thinking it was some sort of trick by the adults.

"Perhaps," Tricks whispered to me, "he's been sent by the girls in the secondary school."

Unlikely, I thought. What did the old geezer mean by 'get moving' anyway? Moving where like? The only place I wanted to go was out of there. And fast like!

"I can see that you are all a little confused and a good deal frightened by my arrival, but –"

"Other way round more like," I whispered to Kegs, who then did his best to ignore me.

Sir Raphael Bombast Penhaligan fixed me with a stare. "– but it is of vital importance that I speak to you. The future of the world is in your hands and we need your help."

"Right on, head." Atlas nodded his own in a really cool way.

"I am also re . . . re . . . ready to be of assistance." Jambo spoke in a really, really deep voice.

"Me too," Cissy added.

What were they all on about? This was all getting seriously out of hand. Really heavy-duty stuff like!

"*Mzuri sana* (Swahili for thank you), Mister Kitangiri and you too, Miss Hourihan and Mister Malone. I hope when I've finished my story that all of you will feel the same." Sir Raphael Bombast Penhaligan stepped out of the big wooden clogs he was wearing and sat cross-legged on the teacher's desk, facing us. "My nephew and I are members of an ancient family who have lived in Tintagel in Cornwall for thousands of years. I am now the head of the family and although people call me Sir Raphael I want you to call me Puffer. When the rains stopped and the colour of the world began to fade away, my nephew knew that he had to come and get me and bring me to Dripsey before it was too late."

"Why Dripsey? Why us?" I asked.

"You really don't know, do you?" he seemed surprised. We all shook our heads except Sheevra Devine. She was busy looking at her nails.

"Tell us, Puffer," Kegs pleaded.

"A long, long time ago, when the world was very young, there was a meeting of the first peoples, the Nurani, the people of the Light. It was held in Egypt near where the Pyramids now are. These people of the Light, all of whom knew how the history of the world began, were afraid of losing the Secret. It was decided that this Secret, the Secret of the TruthTime, the secret of how it all began, should be written down and hidden safely away."

"Where?" I asked. I was really getting into this like.

"Patience, Mister Sheehan. Patience." Puffer smiled as he suddenly picked up a glass of water and threw it across the room. We all ducked but nothing happened. The glass didn't smash against the wall or anything but seemed to hover in the air. The water that spilt from it then turned into a fine mist. "Watch carefully now!" Puffer said, as he flipped open the lid of a ring on his finger.

There was a beautiful, big diamond hidden in the ring and we could all see it start to glow. Soon a very bright beam came from the ring like a laser pointer. Puffer pointed it towards the mist. The beam of white light first bent into a curve and then changed into the different colours of a beautiful rainbow.

"Wow!" Cissy Hourihan shouted.

"Wicked!" Atlas added.

"Po . . . po . . . powerful magic," Jambo said nervously.

"At that first meeting, the Nurani peoples of the world wondered where to hide the Secret. Suddenly a rainbow appeared in the sky and one of its ends landed very close to where they were sitting. Somebody suggested that this was a sign and that the Secret should be buried where the rainbow had entered the ground. They all agreed. Here it would be safe from evil types who lived in the Badlands and who would use the Secret to hurt others."

"Why would they do that?" Kegs asked.

25

"Secrets are strange things. People can use them for good or evil." Puffer was distracted by his own words for a moment. "TruthTime, is the strangest secret of all."

"Hey, head!"

"Yes, Mister Malone."

"If I was burying a secret then I'd want to remember where I left it and how to get it back." Atlas said what we were all thinking.

"You are right, Mister Malone. It was decided that the colours of the rainbow would be the key to where the Secret lay. This meant however that the colours of the rainbow had to be protected because if they were lost then the rainbow would not form and the Secret would be gone forever. Try and think of the Secret as a wishing-well, full of knowledge, wisdom and goodness."

"And the rainbow as a fountain." It was Cissy who spoke. That girl knew a whole lot more than she ever let on.

"Exactly, Miss Hourihan."

"I still don't understand what it has to do with us." I was puzzled.

"At that first meeting of the Nurani peoples of the Earth, the people of Light who lived in Ireland were represented by the Faery Queen and six leprechauns from the faery-mound of Dripsey. As luck would have it they were put in charge of the rainbow's colours."

"Faeries. I don't believe in faeries," Tricks said bravely.

"Why not, Mister Kirby." Puffer waved his hand and the rainbow in the classroom disappeared. "There are things in the world that we see yet never fully understand so is it not conceivable that the things we cannot see are even less understandable. There are dimensions and moods all around us that only the Secret of TruthTime can explain. Take good and evil for example! There has always been good and evil in the world, in conflict with each other. It's like a balance or the see-

26

saw in the school playground. Sometimes it leans this way . . ."
Puffer was moving his outstretched arms up and down like an
aeroplane's wings. ". . . and sometimes the other. How else do
you explain what's happened to the weather in the last few
years, or fears as you now call them?"

"I dunno." Tricks screwed up his face.

"At the moment the evil dwellers in the Badlands are trying
to take control. It was Skathanna and her twin helpers, the
Salmon Kings (Sounded like a rap band to me!) from the Land
of Shadows who brought the rain. They are from the evil side
and decided that if they could not have the Secret of the
TruthTime, then nobody could and that they would wash the
colour from the world. No more rainbows and therefore the
loss of the Secret. As simple as that! Evil would then invent its
own Secret, its own version of the Truth, and with it overcome
good."

"But what about us? We can still see in colour!" I'd
forgotten all about my pledge.

"Yes, Mister Sheehan, but not for much longer. The Faery
Queen and the leprechauns when given the job of minding the
colours were also told that if they ever lost them they would
only have a short time to get them back otherwise they too
would lose the ability to see and find the colours."

"How long do we have, Puffer?" Tricks spoke up again.

"Seven days."

"And nights?" I asked, thinking it doubled the time.

"Don't be stupid, Bull. You can't find colour in the dark,"
Cissy Hourihan said matter of factly. Puffer nodded.

"Are you telling us that we are leprechauns?" Atlas asked.

I have to say at this point that I didn't fancy the idea of being
dressed in short pants and wearing a stupid cap. The rubber wet
suit didn't seem so bad in comparison.

"Yes, in a way. But you don't have to wear short pants and
caps." Puffer winked at me. I was relieved he could read my

thoughts. "All of you, and Miss Devine, are the next in a long line of guardians of colour that has stretched back through the ages. Mind you none of the others were ever called on to do what you have to do."

"Why did you mention Sheevra Devine separately, Puffer?" I spat out. I could feel my allergy coming on.

"Miss Devine is the Faery Queen." Puffer smiled at Sheevra Devine who was suddenly looking smug. A 'yellow and orange wet suit with red zips' type of smugness. I was beside myself with envy? No, I tell a fib. I was beside Kegs but was still jealous. Not that I wanted, mind, to be a faery queen or anything, like, but Sheevra Devine of all people.

"How come?" I persisted.

"I see that you will all have a lot of questions and I will try to answer them. There is however something I have to do first." Puffer jumped down off the desk. "I want you to gather round me and I'll explain how we are going to go about the business. Gobstoppers anybody?" He pulled a bag of large different-coloured gobstoppers from his pocket and we all took one.

Sucking them kept us from asking him any more questions for a while.

4

THE QUEST (IONS)

⁂〰ᛗ ᚦ◆ᛗ•◆ (ᚻ□■•)

I was quick to finish my gobstopper. Sheevra Devine's smugness was really irritating. That girl really needs a makeover like, I thought.

"Why is Sheevra Devine the Faery Queen?" I slurped through the last juices in my mouth.

"Because her house is built on the old faery-fort. Its as simple as that." Puffer smiled.

"Wha . . . wha . . . what are leprechauns, Mister Puffer?" Jambo hadn't sucked on his gobstopper much, just licked its edges as if it might be poison.

"A good question, Mister Kitangiri? In the beginning when the peoples of the Faery World and our world lived happily together –"

"The Faery World. What is it?" Kegs interrupted.

"The Faery World is the exact same as this world only everything is a hundred times better and worse, a hundred times louder and quieter and a hundred times brighter and darker. It's a place where everything we as humans have ever achieved, ever had, ever wished for, is held onto and cherished. There is no past, no present and no future. There just is **Is!**"

"**Is** is everything. Wicked!" Atlas interrupted.

"The Faery World still has the colours of the rainbow and that is where you must go to get them back," Bolus added.

"Where is it at?" I asked.

"All around you, Mister Sheehan, but in a different dimension. You cannot see it because the Faery World is protected by walls made of Time." Puffer waved his hand again and the rainbow reappeared. It was like looking into a mirror. We could see ourselves in a reflection beneath the curve of colours.

"How are we supposed to get there, head?" Atlas asked.

"There is a passage and as it happens, Mister Malone you already know where that is!"

"I do!"

"Yes. But first let me answer Mister Kitangiri's question about leprechauns. When the first peoples decided that the Faery World should protect the Secret of TruthTime they needed some of the faeries to remain in our world to do so. Some people today think that leprechauns are faery shoemakers, by insisting that the word means 'little shoe'. In fact when all the languages in the world were being developed many early peoples tended to use images they found in nature to describe things. The original word was actually *Lap-Ra-Kaouan*. It comes from Egypt, where the first meeting of the Nurani was held.

Lap is a word for a blow or hit and *Ra* is a very old, Egyptian word for the Sun. When you put these together as 'lap-ra' it meant the rainbow because the people of long ago saw the rainbow as the sun's way of hitting the earth. '*Kaouan*', on the otherhand, is a word that described the fierce noise that the birds known as stone-curlews made in the marshes of Egypt when hunters were about. Amongst the Celtic peoples the word imitated the loud shriek that tawny or screech-owls make when they want to let other animals and birds know that there is danger in the forest. Normally their call is 'kewick' but when disturbed it became '*kaouan*'. Say it like this! *Cow – un.*"

30

"Cow-un, kaouan, **kaouan**, **kaouan**," we all squeaked in high-pitched voices (All except Jambo, whose voice had broken).

"Because of the racket they made when disturbed, the screech-owls became known as guardians of the forest. For the same reason the people of Light from Ireland who were given the job of looking after the colours of the rainbow were soon being called '*Lep-ra-kaouns*', the alert guardians of the sun's blows, or colours that made up the rainbow." Puffer held his hands out. "You are now the next in a long line of leprechaun guardians."

"As long as we definitely don't have to dress up in short pants and stupid jackets like," I said.

"No. I assure you. You are what you are!" Puffer pointed to our reflections in the mirror of mist.

"That's very deep, head," Atlas added.

"Wha . . . wha . . . what are you so?" Jambo looked at Puffer. His concern about evil-spirits and powerful magic made him a bit suspicious of people stranger than he was.

"I am just a guide, somebody to point you in the right direction to recover the colours of the rainbow. When they are all found I will be there to show you how to put them back together again."

"I'd worry so, particularly if they way you dress is anything to go by," I said, a bit cheekily.

"You noticed that, did you, Mister Sheehan? Well the way I'm dressed is deliberate. I am what you might call a colour test card. I needed to be sure that each of you all could still see the colours. I know from most of your thoughts on how I am dressed that you can."

"Most of us, Puffer. What do you mean?" I asked.

"I'm having trouble reading Miss Hourihan's thoughts. There is a lot of interference. It's unusual for a person of my skill, but not unheard of." Puffer looked at Cissy Hourihan whose eyebrows lifted a little. She didn't smile or get embarrassed.

"I can see all the colours, Puffer. You don't have to worry," she said snootily. Puffer just nodded his head, but to me, at any rate, he looked a little worried.

"Are we all going to go after the colours together or are we just going to get one each? There are seven of us." Sheevra Devine spoke in a very posh and superior voice.

"Yes and no. You will start by travelling together but each of you can only recover one of the colours, and when you *do* you have to return with the colour. There will be one opportunity and one opportunity only for a person to return with two colours. The last person will be on their own, I'm afraid."

"How do we know which colour?" Kegs asked.

"You have already chosen!" Puffer giggled as he waved away the rainbow.

"How?" Tricks asked.

"Look at your tongues." Puffer laughed.

We all looked at each other's tongues. They were coloured from the gobstoppers and each of our tongues was a different colour. To be sure we rushed out to look in the bathroom mirror. Atlas' tongue was red, Sheevra's was orange, Keg's yellow, Jambo's green, Trick's blue, Cissy's was indigo, and mine violet. Puffer was still laughing when we came back in.

"How do we get to the Faery World?" Sheevra asked, slightly annoyed that as the Faery Queen she didn't already know.

"You already have an inkling. Please stand in front of the map." Puffer pointed to the map on the wall. "Do you remember the place that never got wet?"

"Timbuktu!" I shouted. I just knew there was something strange about that dry spot.

"Exactly, Mister Sheehan. When it is time to go you will all place your hands, one on top of another, over that spot and the Time Hole will open up. You will then be in Faery World and will travel to different parts of it to find the colours."

"Ho . . . ho . . . how?" Jambo was suspicious again. His family were stuck in a container for a long time when they came to Ireland first and he was never going to travel again without being fully sure of how or where he was going.

"A *whirlwind*," Cissy Hourihan said.

We all looked at Puffer.

"That's right, Miss Hourihan. I must say I'm might'ly impressed by your knowledge. Faeries use whirlwinds for transporting themselves, almost like a tornado that sucks you from one place to another."

"I'm not so sure about that. I've my hair to think about." Sheevra Devine tossed her head back as she spoke. "These extensions were very expensive."

Between her false hair, false nails and fake belly-ring, Sheevra Devine was a 'Get real!' nightmare.

"You'll find it's not as bad a way of travelling as you think." Puffer calmed her down.

"Right. Let's go!" Kegs shouted as he went towards the map.

"Hold it, Mister Murphy! First we need to take some precautions."

"What do you mean?" I asked.

"Where you are going is dangerous as well as exciting. You have seven journeys to make and each will be difficult. You will all need some special equipment to make it easier. Tricks of the trade if you like."

"What kind of tricks?" Tricks asked.

Puffer pulled from his pockets seven mobile phones and placed them in a row on Mister Penhaligan's desk. Each of the phones was a different colour, to match our tongues.

"Wicked! Just like a rainbow," I said, as I looked at them.

They were the very latest model, built from titanium and completely shock-proof. I'd heard from my older brother that you could play soccer with them if you wanted. Now, needless to say like, I've always wanted a mobile phone but my parents wouldn't let me have one.

"I suppose they're alright." Sheevra Devine said dismissively. She, of course, had one already, but of the older type thankfully.

"These are for communication with me and each other. In Faery Land the sound signals are distorted by time so you will have to learn the Fairy-Dimension Texting Language (**FDTL**). This is very like the Windings language used by some computers, but it is able to overcome the warping between dimensions. For example when you want to call up a whirlwind for transport you type in '⚕︎〰︎〉〈☐●◆〉〈■Ω' or '⚕︎⚕︎Ω' for short."

"Heh, head. Wicked, man!" I think Atlas was pleased. Sometimes it was difficult to know for sure.

"Why not video phones? Wouldn't it be better if we could see each other as well," Sheevra asked. That girl dreamt about accessories when the rest of us settled for the occasional nightmare.

"Unfortunately you are leaving a land of black and white to enter one of colour. The amount of battery time required for the phones to make that change when relaying signals is too great. Keep things simple! Sound is enough." Puffer smiled indulgently.

Too right! I thought. I was not sure that I wanted to see Sheevra Devine unless I had to.

"I sense from what you have just said, Mister Puffer, that you do not intend to travel with us." Jambo sang out this long question.

We all looked at Puffer.

"No. I'm not. I'm unable to pass into Faery Land so you will have to do it on your own."

FAIRY DIMENSION TEXTING LANGUAGE

ABCDEFGHIJKI

"What will we tell our parents?" Sheevra asked. "My mother will want to know."

"They will not notice the time you are gone because, once through the Time Hole you leave behind this world and when you return it will be only a few moments after the time you left.

You can say you are helping Mister Penhaligan to tidy up the school before it's closed. That won't be too much of a lie. You are helping."

"Yeah, that's right. We are. Let's go!" Tricks was ready.

"Not so fast, Mister Kirby. There is much you need to learn first and I haven't told you about the wish you each have yet."

"A wish for all of us?" Cissy asked.

"Yes. Because of the difficulties that lie ahead each of you has one wish."

"Great. I'd like a –" Kegs began to blurt out.

Puffer held up his hand with a cross look. "*Stop* right there, Mister Murphy, right now! The wish can only be used to help someone else and not yourself. The individual colours of the rainbow are of no use on their own and it is only when they are together that the light will return. It is the same for you seven. You are now the seekers and must depend on each other to find the way. However you must be very careful when you use the wishes to help each other because they will be needed."

"That's ridiculous." Sheevra's face pouted. She had never had a wish denied to her before.

"Perhaps, but it is as it is. Now if you are ready to start learning what you need to know we can get started. There is much to understand."

"Go for it, head. Get us in the groove, man." Atlas was grinning stupidly but we all nodded our heads as well.

But, I wondered, did we really know what we were getting ourselves into? Tricks didn't seem bothered and was already asking if I would swap wishes with him.

5

THE FIRST JOURNEY

⁂〜ℳ ☞⊁⌂⬧⬧ ☺⌂⬥⌂■ℳ⬔

We were all really happy that it was Atlas who was going after the first colour. If he got back with his colour alright, then he would be able to help the rest of us find the other places by using the mobile phones.

Before I go any further I'd better tell you a little bit more about Atlas Malone. He was the biggest of us lads, but not as tall as Cissy, with black bushy hair and a pink birthmark in the shape of a butterfly on the back of his neck. His parents were 'crusty-veggies' and made cheese from goat's milk to sell in the market. He had one brother who was about seven fears older than him and who was meant to have, what the teachers called, an attitude problem.

Atlas used to joke that what his brother really had was an *'altitude'* problem, in that his brother just didn't like coming out on top of the class. He had to change schools about three or four times and was now doing some 'stuff' in Amsterdam.

I sometimes worried about Atlas and wondered what he really meant when he talked about the presents he got from his brother in Holland. 'Hash instead of cash every birthday, head. Wicked, man!'

On the grey after Puffer Penhaligan first came to the school we were all ready and waiting beside the map for Atlas to arrive. He said he had to go to the bicycle shed to lock up his bike and he seemed out of breath when he eventually came.

"Right then. Are you all ready?' Puffer asked.

"Yeah!" We all nodded nervously.

"Any last-minute requests." He didn't look us in the eye when he said this.

· "No, head. Have you any last-minute instructions?" Atlas asked. I wished they'd stop using words like 'last-minute'.

"Yes, I do, as it happens," Puffer answered, in a serious tone of voice. "Remember, on any single adventure to recover a colour, you may only use the whirlwind for the two journeys away from and back to the school. Also, and very importantly, you may only use one of your wishes in each adventure. Don't waste them. Understand?"

"Yeah," we all mumbled.

"Telephones on?" he asked. We nodded once more. I wanted to go to the toilet again. "Remember Mister Malone, when you get to the other side ask for a man called Bolus. It is he who will lead you to the first colour."

"Right, head. Gotcha man!" Atlas looked as if he was dreaming but was the first to place his hand on Timbuktu. One after another we all did the same and when Kegs, who wanted to go last for luck, put his hand on mine a strange sound started up but then just as quickly stopped.

"Wha . . . wha . . . what's happening?" Jambo asked.

"I'm sorry. As the first hand to go on the map, Mister Malone must be the one to type in the password on his phone. On the way back, remember to do it in Fairy-Dimension Texting Language." Puffer was a bit flustered.

"What is the password, head?" Atlas asked.

"Raincolour."

We all unravelled while Atlas pulled out the phone from his pocket. Once he had typed in the password, we then quickly placed our hands back on the map. The sound started up once more. It was like a dentist's drill, and it got louder and louder. It got so loud that my teeth were rattling like.

"Don't worry." I could just about hear Puffer shouting. "The door hasn't been opened for a long, long time and it's rusty."

Suddenly, the map, then the wall, and then it seemed like, the whole building, started slowly turning around our hands.

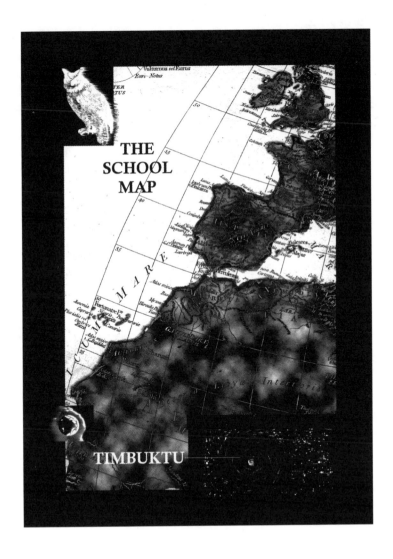

'Stay together!' were the last words from Puffer I heard. The turning got faster, and faster and faster. It felt warm. We were being sucked into a tunnel whose sides were made of flashing, circling lights. Puffer had said it would be like going in for one of those special tests in the hospital where they can see all your insides. You're put you on a trolley and rolled into the tunnel of a machine that takes photographs.

"I always wanted a picture of my brain," Kegs had said when hearing this.

"Why? You don't have one!" Tricks had laughed.

Nobody was laughing now as the walls whirled and whirled around us. It went on for ages like, and if you moved a little and touched the wall by accident sparks would fly.

Suddenly it stopped and we found ourselves in a room just like the one we had left but Puffer or Mister Penhaligan weren't there. It was really bright like, so bright it almost hurt your eyes. I could smell sausages cooking and there was music playing. There were children's voices laughing and when we went to the window and looked out there were funnily dressed kids playing chase in the yard.

There was a woman looking after them. She turned to look at us, smiled and told us to come on out. When I looked at her I didn't know whether she was young or old, as she seemed to change from moment to moment. When we walked it was like walking on air or as if we were wearing really springy shoes. We all went outside. The sky was a golden colour and the grass was blue. The woman was facing away from us but her head seemed to be able to swivel fully so that her head was back to front to smile at us. It was a really weird scene, like. She had long, golden hair, small little ears and a staring smile.

"You are welcome friends from the other side. My name is Shimmer. How can I help you?" she asked.

"We're looking for a man called Bolus," Sheevra Devine

40

said poshly. "Please show us the way if you don't mind. We are in a hurry you know."

"The Sweetmaker, the Soapmaker, the Astronomer, or the Tincture maker?" The shimmering woman looked at us all, waiting for an answer. We didn't have a clue like. Puffer had said nothing about this.

"Are you saying there are three or four people with the same name?" Cissy asked.

"No!"

"Then wh . . . wh . . . why did you ask whi . . . whi . . . which of the gentlemen we . . . we . . . we're looking for?" Jambo stuttered. He was always nervous around new people.

"I didn't. Here in Faery World you will learn that people or things are known not only by their names but also by their moods. When you go looking for someone you have to know what mood they're in, otherwise you won't find what you're looking for. What mood do you want?"

"Hey, head. This is complicated man. Hold on for a moment please, lady. Lads gather round!" Atlas pulled us all into a tight circle and whispered, "This is as good a time as any to try out the phones. Text Puffer and ask him."

"I'll do it," Cissy said and tapped in the question in Fairy-Dimension Texting Language on her phone. The answer soon came back.

"Wha . . . wha . . . what does it announce?" Jambo asked.

'❄︎〰︎ⅿ︎☐ⅿ︎ ⅄⬩ ☐■●⬡ ☐■ⅿ︎ ○☐☐■,' it read.

"There is only one moon," Cissy translated.

Atlas looked puzzled for a moment but then copped what had happened.

"Listen, head. I think you asked him about moon instead of mood. Send it again!" he said quietly but firmly.

"Sorry. Silly of me," she replied, a little embarrassed.

I'd never known Cissy Hourihan to have ever been silly, much less admit it. She tapped out the question again and after

41

a few moments and some strange noises the reply flashed. We all looked over her shoulder to read it.

'❦ ▢▢◆ ♌▢⧓●⧓■℣ ◯▢▢♎ – a pot boiling mood –,' it read.

"Puffer must mean sweets, hard-boiled sweets," Atlas said. "I know because Tiffany and Tobias – Atlas always called his parents by their first names – make hard-boiled, watercress and mint sweets for sale in the market."

"Sounds cool." We all nodded in agreement.

"The Sweetmaker please, Miss Shimmer," I turned to say to the woman but she was gone.

The children were gone and the only thing left in the yard was a screech-owl sitting on the gate. Its body was facing away from us but its head was swivelled completely so that its slowly blinking eyes could watch us carefully.

"*Cow-un, cow-un.*" It suddenly screeched and launched itself into the air. It flew round and around in circles, until we realised that the owl wanted us to follow it.

And follow it we did, down the road into the town. The town itself was almost exactly like Dripsey except that the walls were all made of glass. Sheevra Devine kept looking at her reflection, smiling admiringly. You could see people inside who smiled out at us. The roofs were made of leaves instead of tiles. When you looked closely at the people inside they looked exactly like the people we knew from home, except happier. It was really weird like.

The owl screeched to a halt at a shop door before darting inside. There was a large sign flashing in the window.

Bolus Mendez.
POT BOILER
EXTRAORDINAIRE.

We all went in after the owl. Everywhere were shelves of different-coloured marshmallows, gobstoppers, fizzy drops and winegums. There were buckets of jellybabies and strings of liquorice hanging from the roof-beams. A man who looked very like Puffer stood behind the counter. He wore a crispy clean apron and a white trilby hat.

"What can I do for you friends?" He asked.

"We're looking for Bolus," Tricks asked.

"Why?" He replied.

"We've lost the colour red from our world and we need his help to find it," I said.

Suddenly, and I mean right away like, everything in the shop changed. The glass walls became like cold stone. The shelves of marshmallows and gobstoppers and fizzy drops disappeared and instead there were weird insects and bits of fur and lumps of rock. The buckets of jellybabies were now full of eyeballs that stared up at us. The strings of liquorice changed to hanging bats that darted down and plucked at our hair.

"You're lucky that I'm a very moody person and can change easily. You must be looking for Bolus the Tincture maker," the old man said. His clothes had changed and looked torn and ragged. His hair was all frizzy like Jambo's, and his face was blackened with soot.

"Yes," Cissy said bluntly as she caught a bat and began stroking its neck. I swear on my new mobile phone that it started purring like a cat.

"Then that's me. I'm Bolus and I am now in a chill-out Tincture mood."

"Wicked shop, head. Show us how to get the colour red." Atlas was poking at the eyeballs seeing if they'd float back to the surface when he pushed them under. He stopped when one of the eyes winked back at him.

"You will have to travel far and wide and yet not travel at all to find it," Bolus said. "Red is the last work of the great alchemist."

"Wha'da'ya mean by that?" Kegs said. All of us were puzzled.

43

"One colour delights in another colour; one colour triumphs over another colour; one colour dominates another colour. The colour of red is the wormstone of all the others. It is the lion whose roar frightens the others." Bolus Mendez spoke in a cackling voice as he began pulling down some very old books from a shelf behind him. "We have much to do if you want the colour red but first I musk ask the seeker why it is he wants the colour red. Who is the Seeker amongst you, there can only be one?"

We all looked at Atlas who stepped forward. "I am, head," he said proudly.

6

THE COLOUR RED

♒︎〜♏︎   ♍︎□●□◆□   ◇♏︎♎︎

Part 1. Bolus Mendez

Bolus Mendez came around from behind the counter and stood looking down at us. He definitely was like Puffer, only didn't have the moving wrinkles and his nose was a bit bigger.

"What is your name lad?" he asked Atlas.

"Mickey Malone, head. Me mates calls me Atlas," Atlas replied, standing up to his full height.

"I can see that your heart is strong and brave. You are the map reader, no?"

"Right on, head! Got it in one, dude." Atlas, winks back at us.

Suddenly, Bolus Mendez lets out a roar. We all jump back with the fright. He grabs Atlas by the collar and lifts him so that their eyes are at the same level.

"Do you want your eyeballs to join the others in the barrel, Mister Mickey Malone?" The tinture man's chill-out mood was changing fast.

"No. No siiiiirrrrr!" Atlas stuttered. He was frightened.

"Good. Then refrain from calling me head or dude. I am Bolus. No more, no less. Is that understood?"

"Yesssssss sir, Bolus sir," Atlas squeeked.

"Why did you come here, lad? To help the world you live in?" Bolus squinted.

"Eh . . . yes. Yes of course, sir," Atlas whimpered.

"The truth, lad! Tell me the truth." Bolus began to shake Atlas like mad.

"For the excitement, sir. Nothing else," Atlas admitted after a lot of shaking.

"Good, that's better. There is never any reason to be afraid of the truth. In fact it can set you free. Now tell me why you chose the colour red." He let Atlas down with a thump.

"I don't know," Atlas whispered. "It chose me."

"Look into your heart, lad. Find the reason otherwise I cannot help you."

There was a long silence. The owl blinked and blinked. You could just hear the breathing. Atlas first looked at us and then down at his hands. Small tears were forming in his eyes.

"I think . . ." He hesitated.

"Go on lad!" Bolus smiled for the first time.

"I think it's because I'm angry inside. I'm angry all the time. It eats away at me. It's like an energy taking over my body getting me to do things that are dangerous. I don't know why. I just like things to happen quickly and I get cross when they don't." This was the longest time I'd ever heard Atlas speak for.

"You want to grow up quickly like your brother," Bolus said softly.

"Yes. How did you know that? I hate being a child and being told what to do by teachers and parents. I really hate it." Atlas hands were clenched into a fist. His knuckles where white.

"I was like you, lad. I was in such a terrible rush to get old that I sometimes forgot how nice it was to be young. You never get these times back, you know. If there is any advice that old Bolus can give it's this. Take all that negative energy of yours and let it explode into something creative, something that makes you feel good. In that way your childhood will fly by." Bolus paused to put his hand on Atlas' shoulder. "Is there something that you really like doing?"

16 3 2 13
5 10 11 8
9 6 7 12
4 15 14 1

The Magic Square

OUTSIDE
BOLUS MENDEZ's SHOP

"Yeah! I like to make music. Head banging music." Atlas grinned.

Bolus laughed out loud. So loud it caused the walls to shudder and the owl to screech from its perch.

"Red is definitely your colour, lad. Now let's see if we can find it for you." Bolus was still smiling as he turned and opened one of the large books he had taken down from the shelf. After a few mutters and some minutes he eventually found what he was looking for. "Here it is." He tapped on a page. "The Red of Light. Let me see what we have to do." There was another long silence. "Oh dear!"

"What's wrong, head?" Atlas asked.

Bolus said nothing as he bent more and more over the book to read. Suddenly he let out a large, noisy and seriously smelly fart causing Sheevra Devine to curl up her nose in disgust. The rest of us giggled.

"Sorry about that. I had rat-tail and weevil-bean stew for lunch. Tut, tut, tut, tut. This is going to be very difficult." Bolus lifted up the book and turned back again to look at Atlas. "I've never done it before."

"Never! How come, head?" Atlas asked.

"Never had to! Nobody has ever asked . . . until now." Bolus shrugged his shoulders.

"But what will we do so?" Tricks asked from beside me as he kept one eye on the eyeballs in the bucket.

"We will try?" Bolus closed the book. Dust flew everywhere.

"Tell us what you need," Atlas said.

"Let me see." Bolus walked around the shop looking at the shelves. "Mercury, copper, the essence of Kermes resin, iron, red lead, sulphur, tin, dragons-blood, vinegar, fresh juice of turnsole, root of the brazil tree, madder, crushed cochineal crusts, oil of lilies, crystal of sand, and last but not least the sweat from a pig's back. They are all here. We just need to work out the secret formula."

"I'm not touching any pigs' sweat," Sheevra Devine spat.

"What secret formula?" I asked.

Bolus opened the book and read it very slowly.

'There are sixteen of us, no more.
We'd rather be thirty-four.
For when the proportions are right,
You'll see the Red of Light,
In twenty lines of four.'

48

"It's a riddle," Tricks said quietly.

"Yes," Bolus agreed.

"Wha . . . wha . . . what does it mean?" Jambo asked.

"There are sixteen ingredients and twenty formulas or combinations of the ingredients but the last line is a hint. You only need four at any one time to make the colour red but they must be in the right proportions or amounts. However in order to make the Red of Light, all of the reds must then be mixed together. Each ingredient is numbered and that is the amount of it you must use. When you add the parts together then they must equal 34. Oh dear! I was never very good at maths puzzles." Bolus was scratching his bottom. He seemed to do that when he needed to think.

"It's the magic square. I know it." Cissy Hourihan spoke. All our mouths opened in surprise including that of Bolus whose teeth seemed to move.

"Of course my girl. How did I forget?" he shouted excitedly.

"Show us, Cissy," Atlas said.

Cissy Hourihan put her finger in the barrel of eyeballs and wet it. She then started to draw out numbers in the dust on the floor of the shop.

16	3	2	13
5	10	11	8
9	6	7	12
4	15	14	1

"No matter what way you add them up, including diagonally you get 34. Eight straight lines of four! Two diagonal lines of four and then four squares made up of the corner numbers, the second numbers in each line, the third numbers in each line and the four numbers in the middle. Then there are the four small corner squares of the four numbers in the corner of the big square. Finally there are the rectangles of opposites. The

49

middle two numbers of each line are added to their opposite two. All add up to 34 and these are the twenty ways you can make the colour red from sixteen different ingredients," she said, matter of factly. *(See all these at the back of the book.)*

"Brilliant, young lady. Brilliant! There's a job here for you any time you want." Bolus was dancing.

"Thanks. I'll think about it." Cissy didn't seem that fussed about the offer.

"Let's try the first combination. Top line left to right! Sixteen parts of pigs' sweat, three parts copper, two parts essence of Kermes resin, thirteen parts crushed cochinal insect crusts." He was rushing round the shop picking out the ingredients.

"Go into my workshop at the back and stoke up the fire," he said to Atlas.

"Get me a big, glass bottle from the press over there," he said to Kegs. "In fact get twenty of them and one extra for luck."

"Get twenty of the eyeballs from the bucket. We will use them as stoppers on the bottles and they can keep a close eye on the mixtures. Heh! Heh!" he said to Tricks who wasn't that keen about sticking his hand into the bucket.

"I want you to check on my mood sign and then put a 'do not disturb notice' on the door," he said to Jambo.

Jambo went outside the shop and a after a few seconds came back in.

"What does it say?" Bolus asked.

"Bo . . Bo . . Bolus Mendez. Tincture Maker to the Stars," Jambo replied.

"Good, I'm in the mood! Feed the bats," he said to me.

"Get a life!" he said to Sheevra.

Bolus Mendez was fierce excited like, and Cissy had to follow him round the shop collecting the ingredients as he pulled them down.

7

THE COLOUR RED

⁕〰〰ℳ ℳ□●□◆□ ☼ℳ♎

Part 2. The Poisoning

The next few cowers – hours in the old Before-Rain Language – were a frantic commotion of pounding stones, hissing beakers, spitting spouts, bubbling pots, sparking fires, gurgling tubes and frazzled people.

The first formula was quick to get together and worked right away. After only a few minutes we had a beautiful, red colour sitting in a glass bottle with an eyeball stopper watching it carefully. As the grey went on however, the formulas became more difficult and longer to do but, one by one, more and more bottles of red powder joined the line on Bolus' kitchen table. Soon there were nearly twenty. All the red colours seemed to be the same and yet were different. It was as if each of them had a life of its own like.

Our luck couldn't last and it didn't.

We were at the last formula, the most difficult to prepare, of the four ingredients in the centre of the magic square.

"Ten parts of fresh juice of the turnsole, eleven parts of the root of the brazil tree, six parts of sulphur, and seven parts of tin." Jambo sang out the formula while heating the mixture in the workshop.

The rest of us, including Bolus, had had to get out of the heat and were sucking sweets in the fresh air of the herb garden behind the shop.

Every now and then we would all shout, 'Are you *reddy* in there yet Jambo,' and burst out laughing. Reddy, do you get it? It was sort of an in-house joke whenever the next formula was ready for bottling. We were getting pretty pathetic with our jokes, probably because we were all knackered like. We had worked through the night and in two cowers the sun would come out again. At the time it seemed very funny.

Suddenly, there was an almighty explosion and between the screeching owl and purring bats the place was in an uproar. We rushed in to see poor Jambo holding a broken beaker in one hand, the eyeball stopper in the other and with red powder covering his face and hair. Thankfully, none of the other bottles were broken although the eyeballs had a worried look. We were laughing when he started to choke.

He was going a black type of bluer and bluer as he held his throat. He couldn't breath. The eyeball in his hand stopped winking.

"What's happening?" I shouted.

"Let me see." Bolus pushed us aside. He knelt down to smell the powder covering Jambo before sticking his very long tongue out to taste it. Jambo looked very frightened as Bolus whispered, "It is poison and with all my magic I will not be able to save him in time."

"Atlas. Your wish! Use your wish," I shouted.

He looked at me for a few seconds, hesitating. Jambo had stopped moving. Bolus was feeling his pulse and shaking his head.

"Right, head. You're right. I wish that Jambo doesn't die." We all looked down as Atlas wished. Nothing seemed to happen. "Com'on Jambo. Chill out man," Atlas shouted.

Suddenly Jambo started moving, his eyes and the eyeball stopper started blinking. He was able to breathe again and soon was okay.

"Th . . . th . . . thank you, my friend," he said to Atlas.

"It was nuffink, head." Atlas smiled back.

"Wha . . . wha . . . what happened, Mister Bolus?" he asked of the moody chemist.

"You were poisoned Mister Kitangiri. By mistake we used arsenic sulphide instead of ordinary sulphur in that last mixture. They look the same but I just don't know how it happened. I didn't think I had any of it in the shop. Miss Hourihan and I were very careful in getting down all the ingredients. I just don't know. It is all very strange." Bolus was scratching his bottom again.

"Listen, heads. Let's not let this accident stop us now. We're nearly there. Let's do that last formula again and this time with the right ingredients," Atlas said in a very determined way.

We all agreed and a half a cower later the last of the twenty reds joined the others on the kitchen table.

"We are now ready for the final step," Bolus said.

"Which is?" Cissy asked crossly.

I didn't know why she was so cross as I thought that all the hokem-pokem stuff was right up her ally. The screech-owl sitting on a top shelf glared at her. I don't think they were seeing eye-to-eye with each other like.

Bolus opened the book again and began to read once more.

'Seeker!
Catch the sun's first rays,
in the mist of delight;
and from the twenty,
will be the Red of Light.'

"Another riddle!" Tricks said.

"Delight, delight. I wonder what that means. Tut, tut. My poor old brain." Bolus was walking round and round the room as he thought, scratching and scratching his bottom. Suddenly he stopped scratching. "I have it. I have it!" he shouted. "Delight. Turkish delight. Mist. We need a Turkish bath. We must have steam, loads of steam. Ladies and gentlemen put as many kettles on the fire as possible." He was digging in the presses and throwing as many old kettles as he could find into the centre of the kitchen.

"Explain the riddle, Bolus. Please," Sheevra Devine asked.

"We create as much steam as we can and then we throw all the red powders we have made into the mist where they will mix. The sun's first rays will then cause the different powders in the mix to fuse together and thus we will have the Red Tincture of Light." He stopped explaining to look at Atlas. "You, Mister Malone, must be ready to catch it as the drops form. We don't have much time. The sun will be up in twenty minutes."

And so it happened. We created a red mist in the steam and when the sun came up droplets of the most beautiful red colour were to be seen floating in the air. Atlas rushed around catching them in a special thermos flask that Bolus had given him. Once the last droplet had been caught he screwed the lid on as tight as he could.

"Time to go home," Atlas said, holding up the flask.

"Yeah," we replied.

"Wha . . . wha . . . what do we do?" asked a relieved Jambo.

"Follow the owl back to the school and join your hands at the wall," Bolus said.

"Goodbye, Bolus. Thank you so much, head," Atlas said, smiling.

The screech-owl was waiting and we began to follow it out of the shop.

"One moment, Mister Sweeney," Bolus says to me. I waited until the others were halfway up the road.

"Yes, Bolus," I said.

"I still don't know how the poisoning could have happened.

I'm very worried that there are evil forces out to stop your quest. Be very careful," he said in a very grave voice.

"Right. We will. Thanks, Bolus. Bye!" I shouted as I ran after the others.

Once we had reached the school, Atlas typed in ✿❀❍■♏□●□◆□ in FDTL and we covered hands again. Soon the whirlwind tunnel opened and in an instant we were back in the same room but in a different time. Puffer and Mister Penhaligan were waiting for us and clapped loudly when they saw the flask of Red Tincture that Atlas had. The school clock showed that we had only been gone for two minutes. We spent a long time telling them of our adventure and making plans for the next before giving him back our phones. He said that we were not able to take them out of the school.

I didn't get a chance to mention to Puffer about Bolus Mendez's warning to me.

Like I said. We were knackered and headed home to bed like.

8

THE COLOUR ORANGE

꙼ᾟ ꙳▢●▢◆▢ ꙶ▢Ꙩ■Ꙏᾟ

Part 1. Dainty Dante

Puffer was already at the school when Tricks, Jambo, Kegs and I arrived and he was pacing up and down the corridor looking at his watch.

This wasn't any old type of watch like. It was shaped like a ball and hung on a gold chain dangling from his jacket. There was a small button at the top and when you pressed it the cover of the watch opened like a flower to reveal a very small model of the sun surrounded by the earth and other planets. The little balls just seemed to hover there and we couldn't see any wires or things. If you watched very carefully the little balls could be seen moving in circles around the centre. Every now and then, Puffer would open the watch and, after just taking a quick look, could tell the exact time.

"Good morning, gentlemen. Why is Miss Devine taking so long? Where is she?" he asked.

We shrugged our shoulders but knew well what the likely problem was. Sure enough, five minutes later Missus Devine's car, one of the new Black Shadow sports jobs, pulled up outside the school gate. After a few moments Sheevra got out and started up the path. Honest injun, we nearly wet ourselves with laughing when we saw the get up of her.

She had hair extensions that went almost straight up in the

air like antelope horns and which were coloured orange. She also had on a bright orange dress with matching handbag and belt, even brighter orange socks and to cap it all 'day-glo-fluorescent-burn-your-eyes-out' orange high-heeled cowboy boots. I mean, what could you say like.

"You look very bright this morning, Miss Devine." Puffer said with a deadpan face. He wasn't one for showing much emotion and all that happened when he was amused or annoyed was that one or two of the enormous wrinkles on his face would swap positions. It was a neat trick.

"Thank you. I'm not that happy about the earrings. A little small don't you think? My mother insisted," Sheevra said fussily.

Small? *Flaming Norah*. I thought. They were like ruddy great grapefruits, only orange.

"Where's Cissy?" Tricks asked.

"Aaah! We have a small problem there!" Puffer said, looking at the planets of his watch again. "Last night one of her snakes decided to shed its skin. Miss Hourihan felt that this was not a good time to leave it. Apparently her snakes are very attached to their skins and she wanted to share in its slimegrief." He made it sound like dandruff.

"So what happens now?" I asked.

"I've asked Mister Malone to go again," Puffer answered as Atlas burst through the door, a big grin on his face.

"Hiyya, heads," he shouted.

"Ho . . . ho . . . how is that possible?" Jambo asked, not because he didn't want Atlas to come, it's just he didn't like sudden changes in plan.

"Getting back from Faery Land with a colour, Mister Kitangiri, is dependant on the person carrying that colour tapping the password in on their phone. Once it has been used once for this purpose it is useless. However, although Mister Malone's phone is now redundant he may use somebody else's phone to travel. I've got Miss Hourihan's phone here so he can use that to go as well. Now you'd best get going." Puffer handed Cissy's indigo phone to Atlas as he moved into the classroom and towards the wall.

"Excuse me!" Sheevra stomped.

"Yes, Miss Devine." Puffer's wrinkles were swapping places like mad.

"This is my colour! I should be making those kind of decisions." Her hair extensions threatened at any moment to pin Puffer to the map.

"I agree but in this case you are going to need all of Mister Malone's map-reading skills. He will be of great help to you."

"Right on, head. Tell it like it is man." Atlas added with a swagger.

"Ok, I suppose. But I'm in charge." Sheevra pouted before giving the rest of us a dirty look.

"Of course, Miss Devine, of course," Puffer said, relieved. "You have to be very careful though."

"Why?" she asked, in haughty tone.

"The orange that you seek is called the *Real Gar* and it is very like the stuff that nearly poisoned Mister Kitangiri, only it's orange. It's very scarce and hard to find. Remember, even Bolus Mendez didn't think he had it in his shop and there is only one place you can go to get enough of it for our purposes. Touch it and it could cause your hair to stand on end." Puffer's wrinkles nearly completely flattened when he realised what he said and he had to dodge Sheevra's hair extensions again.

"Very funny!" she said, angrily.

"I'm sorry. It was not meant as a joke," he said as he moved out of range. Puffer could move fierce fast for an old geezer like. "Also, if and when you do find it, Miss Devine, put it in a black box because it can fade."

"Where are we going, Puffer and who do we ask for?" I asked. Time was moving on.

"The man you are looking for is called Dainty Dante. I wish you the best of luck. Please come to the wall."

We all moved. Sheevra made a show of pulling out her phone and typing in the password **'Raincolour'**. After placing our hands one on top of each other over Timbuktu the wall began to spin again. The next thing we knew we were in the school garden and Shimmer was waiting for us.

SHIMMER

"Hello, my young friends. Who do you look for this time?" She had difficulty trying not to gawp at Sheevra's get up. It seemed, that even in Faery land there was a limit to what was considered good taste.

"Dainty Dante. What's the password for the whirlwind?" Sheevra demanded.

"Wow!" Shimmer was still gawping. The rest of us cracked up. "No . . . I'm sorry. It's *'Devine Comedy'*."

"Are you trying to be funny?" Sheevra was getting hot under her bright orange collar.

"No. I'm serious," Shimmer said as she turned away to giggle.

"Very well then," Sheevra said testily as she typed in '⚘ℳ❖Ж■ℳ ◊□○ℳ♎☒' and the whirlwind started up.

Once into it, we were whisked away until it stopped in the middle of a huge swamp. The smell was awful and there were mossies everywhere, biting at us. Sheevra's 'day-glo-fluroescent-burn-your-eyes-out' orange cowboy-boots sank into the mud.

"Where are we?" Tricks asked.

"I don't know, head." Atlas shook his own.

"Look over there!" Jambo shouted.

Coming out of a bank of dense fog was a man with long hair and a flat cap. He came right up to us but didn't look at anyone except Sheevra. Like Bolus Mendez before, he reminded me a lot of Puffer.

"Beatrice. My Beatrice! You have come to save me. I knew you would," the flat cap said excitedly as he knelt down in front of Sheevra.

"I'm not Beatrice. My name is Sheevra. Who are you?" she pouted while trying to extract her boots.

"You're not Beatrice. You look so like my Beatrice. The *mal aeria* is confusing my brain."

"What's *mal aeria*?" I whispered to the others.

"Bad air, from the swamps. It's what, in the old time, people thought caused malaria. We now know it's caused by the bite of the mosquito insect, who live in the swamps," Jambo sang this out, in a really deep voice. "My father still gets the fevers, because where we came from there was a place just like this. The mosquitos lay their eggs in us when they bite and these cause the fevers."

I was sorry I asked like.

"Who are you, I asked." Sheevra insisted, poking her finger into the chest of the kneeling man. One of her boots was finally free from the mud.

"Dainty Dante at your service," flat cap said sadly.

More like Dotty Dainty Dante, I thought.

"Why are you in this swamp?" Kegs asked.

"Because the people in the city would not help protect me from robbers on the road and I was forced to take a shortcut through the swamp." He kept looking at Sheevra, but not in a creepy way.

"What city, head?" Like he said, Atlas always needed to know exactly where he was.

"Venice."

"That's cool, head." Atlas turns to us. "Old city, built on islands, gondolas for taxis, nearly sank completely during the Rains."

"*Jusssssst ooooone cornnnnetttttto!*" Tricks sang really badly. All he knew about Venice was ice-cream.

"Who are you and what do you want?" Dainty Dandy had recovered a little from his disappointment at Miss Orange not being the woman of his dreams.

We told him about our quest and Puffer Penhaligan.

"And what colour do you want my help with?" he asked as he stood up.

"Orange. It's her colour. We have to find stuff called the *Real Gar.*" Kegs pointed to Sheevra.

Dainty Dante looked at her. "Why is orange your colour?"

"Because I'm creative and independent and, although a little moody at times, I'm loyal and lovable."

"Yeah, right!" I sniggered. Sheevra gave me a look that would turn your pee to ice.

"My Beatrice is like that!" Dainty Dante held out his hand to touch her hair.

"Can you help or not?" Sheevra said, trying to pull away. She put one of her 'creative' hands out to stop herself landing on her bottom in the mud. Three 'loyal' false nails were left sticking in it like little 'independent' orange flowers. Her angry face was anything but 'lovable' like.

"Are you sure you are not my Beatrice?" Dainty Dante must have seen more in her than I did. He looked at her for a long time as he splatted a huge mosquito on his arm. Blood squirted everywhere.

"*Flaming Norah!*" I shouted, ducking out of the way, fast as I could like.

"It's the last time I'll tell you. I'm no old fool's fool. My name is Sheevra Devine." Both boots were now free and she stood on firmer ground.

He just shook his head, really puzzled like. "Very well then. Beyond this swamp is the glorious city of Venice. A beautiful city but full of difficult people. You will have to get a gondola to the city from the edge of the swamp. Ask for man called Shylock on the Street of Banks, in the ghetto. That is where you will find your orange, but not in the form you think."

"Wha . . . wha . . . what is a ghetto?" Jambo asked.

"It is a section or quarter of a city where refugees of a different belief or from a different country, from the city's people, are forced to live. They can then be observed and their lives controlled," Dainty Dante replied.

"Oh, like Dri . . . Dri . . . Dripsey is for my family," Jambo said quietly.

62

I looked at him as he stood there. It's funny like, I'd never thought of our town being like that.

Dainty Dante didn't seem to notice. "I will draw you a map because you will need to follow it carefully to get out of the swamp and through the city to his house."

"That's my job, head. Draw me the map, man, and I'll lead these dudes to the house." Atlas pushed Sheevra to one side, much to her annoyance.

Soon Dainty Dante had drawn the map and as we started to say our goodbyes. He looked at Sheevra.

"Be very careful, Beatrice, of the Island of the Dead. Remember, where the Golem is concerned, Truth is dangerous. If you are in difficulty, hide the first and it will all cease."

"I told you. I'm not your bleeding Beatrice!" Sheevra spouted as she stormed off in a flash of orange hair extensions and scattering blood-sucking mosquitos.

Dainty Dante seemed devastated. He shook his head and disappeared back into the fog as sadly, and as lost-looking, as he had come out.

"Com'on, heads, follow . . ." Atlas stopped talking as his phone, Cissy's indigo phone, started ringing. ". . . what's up I wonder."

"Read it, it's probably Puffer," I said.

'✦⌇⋔⬜⋔ ✿ ⇧. ▷●⋔☾◆⋔ ◆⊠◆ ⍥⋔. ☞. "Where R U? Please txt me. F."

"Who's F?" Kegs asked.

"No idea, head. Somebody looking for Cissy maybe?" None of us had any idea. "Probably a wrong number," Atlas added.

We took ages to follow the twisting path out of the swamp but suddenly, after we turned the last corner, we could see ahead of us, across the water, a large city whose buildings seemed to glitter in the sunlight. There was a small jetty at the edge of the swamp and tied up to the barber's pole at the end of it was a big black banana-shaped gondola.

A boy, who was asleep in the boat, jumped up as we shouted out hello.

"Do you want to go to the city?" he asked.

We all nodded and climbed aboard. The boy was about five years older than us and he was wearing a flat straw-hat with blue ribbon, a blue scarf and a white shirt. He untied the gondola and after putting a large oar into the water stood up at the back of the boat and pushed it forward like.

"How much will it cost us?" I asked him. Now this was a stupid question, as we had no money anyways like.

"Nothing. It will be my pleasure."

9

THE COLOUR ORANGE

❋〰ᶬ ☙▢●▢◆▢ ℍ▢☺■ᵛᵒᶬ

Part 2. Shylock

The gondola boy told us his name was Gabbo and that he
lived near the ghetto and the Street of Banks. I think
Sheevra fell in love with him, not because he had a great
personality or anything like, but because he was so coordinated
in his outfit. She had cleaned herself up after the near mud-bath
in the swamp, and spare false nails had been found in the secret
compartment of her bag and fixed in place. She sat at the end
of the boat looking up at him and not at the approaching city.

The rest of us were still wondering why Gabbo hadn't
bothered asking for money when the reason soon became very
clear. As our gondola came near the entrance of the largest and
busiest canal that criss-crossed the city, there was a fierce
amount of all types of boats and ships coming and going. Our
blue-boy Gabbo managed to create more havoc in a few
minutes than I had in my entire life like. He was scraping the
paint off other gondolas, tangling his oar with those of other
gondoliers, butting into jetties and knocking over their barber's
poles.

There were shouts from all around us.

"Go back to the swamp, Gabbo."

"You're not safe in a gondola. Get away from here!"

"Join the army. Fight the Turks. Destroy another place."

"Get a double rowlock and go fishing, Gabbo."

"Get a job on the funeral gondolas where at least you cannot do any more harm to the dead."

We were all dead embarrassed like, and ducked to avoid the smelly sardines that were thrown at us. Being stuck with a learner gondola-driver in the very narrow canals was not easy and we turned up so many dead-end canals that I lost count. I don't think Gabbo had a clue but he and Sheevra seemed to be blissfully unaware of this fact as they continued to admire each other's outfits.

Then a bit of luck happened. Gabbo was looking backwards trying to figure out where he had come from, rather than concentrating on where he was going, when a low footbridge appeared dead ahead. I was about to warn him when Atlas held his finger up to his mouth.

Sure enough as the gondola slipped under the bridge, he was knocked clean off and fell into the water with a massive splash.

Atlas was first to react. "I know how to get to the Street of Banks from here, heads."

Due to his expertise with flotation devices, Kegs was put in charge of the oar. Sheevra wanted to go back for Gabbo, who was happily swimming out to sea rather than for the safety of dry land, but we held a vote and overruled her.

"But I'm in charge. Puffer said so," she spat like a cat.

"Not when it comes to direction, head," Atlas said. "That's my job."

"Jusssssst ooooone diiiiirection! Give it to meeeee!" Tricks sang again, badly.

"Shut up, Tricks," Sheevra said as the rest of us cracked up. She was being a moody orange again.

True to his word, after two lefts, one right, one left and two rights, Atlas's navigation was spot on and we arrived near the Street of Banks in the ghetto. We asked a passer-by where we could find Shylock and were pointed towards the second of a row of seven archway doorways. There was a sign outside.

THE ORANGE BANK
GHETTOBLASTER
FINANCE AND SECURITY

We went inside and crept up to the counter. There was nobody around. The floor and walls were decorated with tile mosaics of strange shapes and symbols. It was dark and a little bit hairy, as in hairs standing up on the back of your neck like. Sheevra pushed down on the counter-bell. The noise of it rolled around the room like an echo.

"Hello, young friends." A hoarse voice spoke suddenly from behind us. "How may I be of service?"

We all jumped with the fright and turned to see who it was. A thin man with old leathery skin and dirty fingernails had been standing in the shadows, quietly watching us. He was wearing a small yellow cap to cover his bald skull and a brown fur-collared cape that dragged off the ground. In one hand he carried a balancing scale, like you'd see in the old films or in horoscope charts for Libra (my star sign). It clinked and rattled as he came forward. We moved aside to let him pass.

"We are looking for a man called Shylock. Dainty Dante sent us," Sheevra said.

"I am Shylock. How is my old friend Dainty?" The old man asked quietly.

"Swamped with affection!" Tricks said with a giggle.

"Wh . . . wh . . . why is this called the Orange Bank?" Jambo, asked.

"There are seven banks on this road and they are all called after the colour of the receipts we give people who leave money with us. The Red Bank, the Yellow Bank and so on! But that's not why you're here, is it?"

"We have come to find the orange of *Real Gar*. Can you help? Dainty Dante said something about a Golem?" Sheevra, said in her superior way.

Suddenly, the room seemed to get very cold as a wind came in from nowhere. The window and doorframes rattled and, I swear, I saw some of the symbols on the walls changing shape. Yer man, Shylock, took a deep breath, which seemed to crackle all the way down to his toes. He sounded like my granny after her morning cigarette.

"Nobody has mentioned that name around here for a long, long time. Do you know what dangers you are letting yourself in for? Is your quest that important?"

"Yes," some of us said with more bravery than brains and once again we told him the story about the loss of colour and how we had come looking for orange.

"Wha . . . wha . . . what is the Golem?" Jambo asked.

"Good question, young man, but you should do something about that stutter." Jambo looked hurt as Shylock continued. "The Golem is everything you want it to be or nothing at all. He is someone you can call on to help you when you are in trouble and who will wreak havoc on your enemies. The Golem is a new person made from clay and the type of person you want him to be will depend on the spell you cast," Shylock said quietly.

"So what do we have to do to get orange?" Sheevra asked.

"The *Real Gar* that you seek is a very special clay that can only be extracted from the ground in one way and that is by making a Golem out of that clay."

"How do we do that?" Sheevra asked.

"First you will have to draw a Tree of Life on the ground above where the *Real Gar* lies hidden. Within the drawing of the Tree, there are ten windows, which are known as the Gates of Light. In some of these windows, according to a secret formula that I will show you, you will have to write magic letters. When all that is done, you then have to pour water onto the Tree drawing, which comes from a well that no one has ever drunk from. In this way you will form the Golem, the spirit man made from the orange clay, who will then come alive." Shylock, was shaking.

"What happens then?" I asked. "How will we get the orange from him?"

"It is hard to be certain, my friend."

"Why?"

"Every Golem is different. He can be used for good or evil but this depends on what's in the heart of the person who created him," Shylock replied, but without looking at me. "You'll have to ask the Golem about the Orange."

"Whe . . . whe . . . where is this clay?" Jambo asked in an earthy way.

"If you stand at the door and look towards the sea, you'll see a small island. That is where you must go."

"Good. It's very close, heads." Atlas had walked to the door and was pleased when he saw the island was very close.

"And the water?" Tricks asked.

Shylock disappeared behind the counter and into the shadows of the building. We could hear him rummaging around in a back room. After a short time he returned and had a black bottle with a large cork stopper in it. You could hear the water sloshing around.

"Here it is. The water from an iceberg." He handed it to Sheevra.

"Thank you," she said politely.

"No! Thank you my young friends," he said with a rattle of his scales.

"For what?" Sheevra asked.

"For the exchange," he said, holding up the scales.

"What exchange?" she wondered.

"My dear young lady, this is a bank, not a gift shop. You

will need to give something in exchange," Shylock said with a greedy glint in his eye. "It's just business."

"Oh. What do you want?" Sheevra sounded nervous.

"Your earrings are appealing." He pointed to the large grapefruits Sheevra had dangling off her ears. He must have been the only one who thought so. "Those and a promise. That will be our bargain."

"No way. They belong to my mother and I'd feel naked without them," Sheevra spat back.

"Keep your shirt on, girl. We need his help," I whispered. I hoped, for all our sakes, she would.

"What type of promise?" Sheevra asked with a suspicious look on her face.

Suddenly the phone in Atlas's pocket went again. He pulled it out and looked at the display. " '✋⊠O ◆⊙)(◆)(■Ⅶ)o. ☞.' I'm waiting. F," he read the message out with a shrug of his shoulders. "Wrong number again, I suppose. Go on with what you were saying, head."

"When you create the Golem, I want a part of him." Shylock was still looking at Sheevra, ignoring the interruption.

"A part! That's gross," she said.

"Which part?" I asked, thinking that if Shylock was asking for a piece, it mustn't matter to the Golem.

"Firstly. Do you agree to this bargain?" He was still looking at Sheevra and his eyes misted over as she jumped right in there.

"Yes. Get on with it, would you. I've a hair appointment back in our world I don't plan on missing," she said testily as she glared at the rest of us. "This is my colour and my decision."

"Which part?" I asked again.

"His strength, what we call his *gevurah* or heart," Shylock said slyly.

This is not good, I thought.

"What are the magic letters?" Tricks asked.

"You must draw the Tree first, like this." Shylock drew out ten circles, which were all linked by straight lines so that it looked like a tree *(See the diagram at the back of the book)*. "The magic letters that you need to make the Golem are E . . . M . . . E . . .T and you write them in these circles here, here, here and here. Nowhere else!"

"What does EMET mean?" Kegs asked.

"EMET means truth. Isn't that what you are looking for, the key to the secret of the TruthTime?"

"Yes," we agreed.

"Ma . . . ma . . . may I ask you one more thing, Mister Shylock?" Jambo was about to leave the Bank when he turned around to look back at the moneylender.

"Of course," Shylock answered.

"Wh . . . wh . . . why do you want the power of the Golem?"

"To help me collect bad debts. As you can see I'm not a strong man and there are many out there who refuse to pay me back the money I've leant them. The Golem will do that for me."

"Why don't you make one for yourself like. You know what to do with all that secret letter stuff," I said, reasonably.

"I've spent many, many lifetimes studying how to form the Golem only to find in the end that I could not do it on my own. I thought my chance had gone but then you came along." Shylock smiled at us.

"Why us?" Kegs asked.

"The Golem can only be created by persons, who have not been contaminated by the evil in our world. Because of the type of work I do, I've met a lot of people who are corrupt and it's hard to avoid getting a little that way yourself. But you, my new friends, as visitors to my world, are pure. With my secrets you can make the Golem." Shylock sounded a little sad as he said this. "You had better be going."

10

THE COLOUR ORANGE

⁂〰〽 ♠□●□◆□ ℍ□☺■〽〽

Part 3. The Golem

The short trip to the island should have only taken ten minutes of rowing in the gondola but there were a huge number of boats heading in the same direction. All of the gondoliers were wearing masks and heavy blankets covered what they were carrying in the boats. We had to wait our turn to land at the small jetty and eventually pulled alongside another gondola and tied up to a barber's pole.

"Why's this place so busy, head?" Atlas shouted to another gondolier who was about to leave the island.

The man looked at him for a moment. "There is disease and plague in the city. The people who have died are brought here to the Island of the Dead for burial," the man answered, in a hurry to get away.

"*The what!*" Sheevra shrieked. "Dainty Dante warned us about this place."

"We don't have much choice if we want to get Orange," Kegs said sensibly.

"What disease?" I shouted at the departing gondolier.

"The Black Death," he replied in a hushed voice.

As we got off the boat I wondered whether the Black Death was anything like the PANDA virus back home.

"Where do we go now?" Kegs asked.

"According to Shylock's map, head, there is a small lighthouse at the end of the island. That's where we must go," Atlas replied as he headed off.

We passed by loads and loads of graves, and men digging hundreds more, before we finally got to the lighthouse. It was at the very end of the huge graveyard and some of the gravediggers blessed themselves when they saw us going up to it. When I say lighthouse I mean it looked like a lighthouse only there wasn't a light or fire on top of it. Instead, there was a big bell that clanged and clanged and clanged every time the gravediggers put another coffin in the ground.

Suddenly the bell stopped as Sheevra took out Shylock's diagram from her bright orange bag. At the same time I noticed that a small book fell out as well. I picked it up.

"THE REALLY ROUGH GUIDE TO POPULARITY." I read its title aloud as I handed it back to her. She went a bright orange-red colour as she quickly put it back in her bag.

"I'll never speak to you again, Bull Sheehan," she said as she started drawing out the circles on the ground.

"A bit of a dodgy book if it's giving you that type of advice," I shot back, smart like. I was thinking 'great'.

"Now for the magic letters."

She ignored me as she finished the secret diagram by joining up the lines connecting the circles in the way that Shylock had shown us.

"E . . . M . . . E . . . T." We all called out as she drew them in the circles he had indicated.

The gravediggers must have heard us and we were suddenly alone in the graveyard as they did a runner. One coffin was left half in and half out of a grave.

"The bottle of water, please." Sheevra looked at Kegs who handed it to her.

She took out the stopper and started pouring some of the clearest blue-green water we'd ever seen. As it hit the ground in the bottom circle the earth began to sizzle and fizzle. A cloud of smoke, like the stuff they make with dry ice at the discos, surrounded us and we could barely see what was happening.

"*Flaming Norah!*" I shouted.

"Spirits protect us!" Jambo muttered as he half covered his eyes with his hands.

Up from the ground grew a head on a thick neck with seaweed for hair. Its eyes were closed and it had a nose with only one nostril. We were shaking as it turned a full circle to follow us walking round. Every now and then the nostril would flare and sniff at the air. After a few minutes of this it began to grow again and soon there were shoulders, arms, a body, and finally legs and feet. This was the Golem. He wasn't that big and his skin was almost transparent. You could see right through him.

"Wicked, look at that, heads!" Atlas was pointing to the Golem's chest where we could see his heart beating away. It was a bright orange blur whereas the rest of his body was a white-clay colour. A fierce ugly looking lump of clay, he was too like. He just stood there, eyes closed and not moving.

"Is that the *Real Gar?*" Sheevra pointed to the orange beating heart.

"I wonder does he talk or what," Tricks whispered, as he plucked up the courage to go up to the Golem and poke him in the ribs.

"Watch out, head!" Atlas screamed. He was looking up at the sky.

We all watched as two dark skull-shaped clouds came thundering up from the sea and began circling the lighthouse. They went round and round, going faster and faster and there were sparks of electricity flying about like you'd see caused by dodgem cars at the funfair. Suddenly, there was a bridge of lightning between the two clouds before the flash twisted, turned towards the ground and hit the Golem on his forehead. As we stood there, our mouths hitting our shoes, we could see writing beginning to appear on the Golem's forehead. There were three more flashes in a row.

"*Flaming Norah!* Look at that," I said as I read out the letters after each flash. "E . . . M . . . E . . . T."

When the T appeared the spinning clouds disappeared and the Golem started to move. His eyelids blinked and then opened to stare at us. We all jumped back.

"Ask him," Tricks said.

"You ask him," Sheevra whimpered.

"It's your colour," Tricks said.

"Oh, very well then. You're all so pathetic really," she sneered before walking towards the Golem. He looked more frightened of her hair extensions than we were. "We need the colour Orange," Shevra demanded.

"Nosh vine wisdom?" he mumbled, having difficulty pronouncing the words at first.

"No."

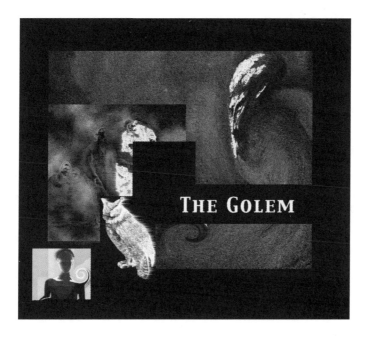

THE GOLEM

"Nosh my greatness?" he added. The Golem's voice got steadily stronger, the mumble soon disappearing.

"No."

"Not my beauty?"

Unlikely like, I thought as I looked at him. He seemed to be getting taller with every passing minute.

"No. I said we want Orange!" Sheevra was getting impatient, and not for the first time.

"Not my force, my *gevurah*." The Golem pointed to his beating orange heart.

"We . . . we . . . well yes!" It was Sheevra's turn to stutter.

"That's mine," a voice suddenly cackled from behind us. We nearly wet ourselves with the surprise. Shylock must have followed us.

"I am able to offer it only once," the Golem said gravely.

"Then it's to me that it will be given," Shylock demanded while looking at Sheevra. "That is our bargain."

"That's unfair," Sheevra whined. "You said he would give us Orange if we made him."

"You have a very short memory, young lady. I said I would help you make him but that you would have to ask the Golem for the Orange. I asked only for one part and that is our bargain. It is unfortunate that we both require the same part but a deal is a deal. You must now honour it."

The Golem was getting bigger and bigger. Soon there was a large hole in the ground from where his body was sucking in new clay. It seemed to travel up the big ugly veins on his legs in clots.

"That's really, really unfair!" Sheevra was stomping up and down in an orange haze.

"I'm very hungry. Be quick with your decision," the Golem growled as he looked at Kegs, and licked his lips.

"This is not good, lads. Whaddda we do now?" Kegs said nervously.

"We . . . we . . . we must think," Jambo said.

"Yeah. Lets go in a huddle and think," Tricks agreed.

We all grouped in a circle to think, looking back every now and then to see what Shylock and, more importantly, what the Golem was up to.

"What did Dainty Dante say to you again, head?" Atlas asked, looking at a seething Sheevra.

"Be very careful of the Island of the Dead. Remember, where the Golem is concerned, Truth is dangerous. If you are in difficulty hide the first and it will all cease." She repeated what Dainty Dante had said. Sheevra had got lots of prizes in our school for reciting poetry. I'd never thought that I would admire her for it but at that moment I did. I resisted hugging her of course.

"Wha . . . wha . . . what did he mean?" Jambo asked.

"Dunno!" Sheevra said nervously.

She had a right to be! The Golem suddenly let out a huge roar, hopped out of his hole and slithered towards us to grab Kegs by his hair.

"What'ya doing?" Kegs screamed. "Let me go, you big lump of muck! Let me gggooooooo!"

The Golem held Kegs up with one hand while another started ripping off his shirt. "If your bargain with the moneylender means giving my heart to him then I will need yours instead. I need a heart, there is no choice."

"Do something, lads. *Quickly*," Kegs began to slobber.

Shylock just stood there rubbing his hands. I looked over at him pleading for help but he just shrugged his shoulders.

Suddenly Trick's face lit up. "I have an idea. I have an idea, lads. I think I've solved the riddle," Tricks blurted out.

"What is it?" Sheevra asked.

"Come here and I'll whisper it to you," Tricks whispered into Sheevra's ear.

This was easy to do because the grapefruit-sized earrings

were back in Shylock's Bank and Tricks could get close. She took ages to cop on to whatever he was saying but then suddenly smiled and nodded her head. She pulled away from the rest of us and walked up to the Golem.

"Mister Golem," she said sweetly. "Let my friend down, I want to give you something instead. If you don't like what it is then you can go ahead and take Kegs' heart."

"*What?* I'll murder you, Sheevra Devine." Kegs was squirming like a fish.

The Golem hesitated for a moment but then did what she asked. Kegs scuttled away like a rabbit and hid behind the lighthouse. The Golem had to kneel down so she could talk to him. "What is it you want?" he growled.

"I made you. Take my heart," Sheevra said in a very quiet voice. She had one hand clenched behind her back and I couldn't figure what was going on.

"I cannot hear you." The Golem stuck a great dirty big finger into muck-filled ears.

"Lean forward and I'll say it again," Sheevra said and the Golem obliged.

"Now! *Now, Sheevra!* Do it," Tricks shouted.

With an orange flash, Sheevra brought her hand round from behind her back and in a quick movement covered over the letter E on the Golem's forehead with her orange glitter lipstick. The Golem made a grab for Sheevra but then stopped as if paralysed.

Nothing else happened . . . for a moment.

"No! Noooooooooo!" Shylock screamed as he ran forward.

Suddenly, in a puff of smoke the Golem disintegrated and disappeared. The hole in the ground filled up in front of our eyes and soon all that was left where he had been kneeling was a small pile of the brightest orange sand you have ever seen. It seemed to glow and dim like his beating heart.

"Wicked, lads!" Kegs shouted as came out from behind the lighthouse.

Shylock was crying as he looked down at the sand.

"How did you do that?" I asked Tricks.

"Don't know. Took a chance. Dainty Dante said remove the first and I guessed he meant the first letter of the word for truth. The E."

Shylock was beside himself as he looked at us. "When . . *sniffle, sniffle* . . . you rubbed out the E from EMET you were left with the word **MET**." By now he was really sobbing. I almost felt sorry for him, but got over it. "**MET** means death and this is the secret way of getting rid of the Golem. That sand there, is the *Real Gar* that you seek."

Sheevra reached into her bag again and pulled out an eyebrow tweezers. Bending down she picked up a single grain of the orange sand in the tweezers and placed it in Shylock's hand.

"Our bargain is honoured, Shylock. You now have one part of the Golem," she said with a haughty voice. "Now leave us alone."

"But . . .but . . ." he whimpered.

"Go, I said. Keep the earrings. I hated them anyway." Sheevra dismissed him with a wave of her hand.

Shylock slunked away from the lighthouse and he must have looked at every single grave as he walked through the graveyard. Every now and then we could hear him moaning.

It took a while, but Sheevra picked up every grain of the orange sand with her tweezers and put them into the black bottle that we had brought the pure water in. Finally finished, she put in the stopper and shouted.

"Come on. Let's get out of here. I'm a mess and I've a hair appointment. I'll call up . . ."

She was interrupted by Atlas's phone ringing again. '❋⌧♦ ✢ ♦○□□□◆. ☞.' 'Txt U tmorrow. F.', was the message. Atlas looked at us, then shrugged and shoved it back in his pocket.

Sheevra had her own phone out and after typing in '**Devine**

Comedy' the whirlwind appeared and we were soon back at the school.

Shimmer was waiting for us and smiled when she saw the bottle full of the *Real Gar* orange.

Funny thing like, I thought, as Sheevra typed in '☼♋⋈■♏◻●◻◆◻' and we put our hands on Timbuktu, in Faery Land we never seemed to get hungry but when we got back to our own side it soon caught up with you.

Now I have a fierce appetite and once I was back in our own school, and had given Puffer a brief account of our adventure, I scattered home as fast as I could to get something to eat.

My mum was not amused, as I had only left the house after breakfast about ten minutes before. She sent me outside to do the chores and clear up some clay that was lying in a heap in our back garden.

I have to tell you that I handled that clay very carefully like.

11

THE COLOUR YELLOW

❄〰︎♏ ♍□●□◆□ ✡♏●●□◆

Part 1. Missus Devine's Tank

When Atlas, Kegs, Tricks, Jambo and I eventually made it to the school again, the next morning, all of us were very edgy. Once inside we huddled around the window and looked back down towards the town.

That morning, the streets of Dripsey – there's only two – were alive with aggro like. On the main street all the farmers were marching, protesting about their animals dying, and on the other smaller street the Coalition Against Television Abuse (CATA) activists were hassling people about what they were doing to the televisions. Norah O'Toole was leading that march and she had chased after me with a sign that said 'Pump up the Volume'. The two groups were going to crash into one another in the centre of the town, where Sergeant Ulysses Finnegan was busy trying to redirect traffic. The mood of people in the town was changing very fast and a lot of stuff was happening.

IL DOCE, the Devine's relative in the Department of the Changing Environment, had come on television the night before and said that the world was facing a major crisis. Animals everywhere were dying from BoCoBSE, the hospitals were full of people with the PANDA virus, and a newer disease called SHAGDED (Shadowtime Always-Going-Dark Eye

Disorder). He made a great show of pretending he was the only one who could solve the problems but that he needed more power.

I read, across the table at breakfast, on the cover of my dad's paper, the *Dripsey Drivel*, headlines saying IL DOCE was considering calling a new government election and putting himself forward as the only leader who had enough vision left to do something. He said he was tired of the riots outside the building where he worked and wanted to put a stop to it. He planned on changing the way the country was run and declaring himself King. He said a strong hand was needed and that he had the support of lots of people including the Army.

I had to laugh at this like, 'cause on the television he wore a purple suit with a green shirt and yellow tie.

My smile didn't last long when, as Tricks and I were watching, we saw the crowds in town scattering as Sheevra Devine's mother ploughed through them and arrived up to the gate of the school driving a tank. It wasn't any old tank like, but one of those new 'Chameleon' stealth types that could sneak undetected by radar across a battlefield and under Sergeant Ulysses Finnegan's huge nose.

Mister Devine was squeezed into a little turret on top, where he kept swivelling the tank's large 'Pacifier' water cannon. The gun was a multipurpose 'Fling-all' type and could be converted into shooting any type of missile you wanted like. It was wicked and we were all jealous.

When Sheevra eventually got out we could see she was wearing a uniform and a peaked cap. She was using one of her old hair extensions like a stick and it was tucked under her arm like a cheerleader's baton. A bit wary of the 'Pacifier' water cannon like, we waited until she came into the school to have a good laugh at her. We all stood in a row and saluted when she entered the classroom.

As usual, Tricks started messing and pulled off her cap so as to try it on. You could have knocked us all over with a feather when we saw what we saw.

"*Flaming Norah*!" I gasped, gobsmacked even. Sheevra's big hair was gone and she was almost bald. "What did you do to yourself?" I asked, looking at the number 1 cut.

"What's with the uniform?" Kegs asked.

"I've been made a captain in the youth section of IL DOCE's new force, the DSS, so I'd advise you to be very careful."

"The what?" Tricks asked.

"Devine's Shadowtime Soldiers. We are to help people get over their fear of the loss of colour and of course help get my relative get elected as King. I'll soon be a princess . . . I'll have you know. A real one and not some stupid Faery Queen." Sheevra said this loudly as Puffer came into the room.

"Have you told your relative about the quest for colour?" he asked in a very serious manner. His wrinkles were changing places like mad.

"No . . . not yet. But I will, if any of you tease me," she said, looking at the rest of us, and Tricks in particular, in a very threatening manner.

There was a loud crashing noise outside. We rushed to the window to see that the gate, and most of the front wall of the schoolyard, had been completely demolished. Missus Devine was having trouble turning the tank around and poor Mister Devine was hanging off the barrel of the gun like a monkey.

"Don't worry, head. I'll keep a close eye on her highness," Atlas whispered in my ear.

"Right! Where are we off to, Puffer?" I said in a happy voice, that I didn't really feel, as we turned away from the window.

"Timbuktu!"

"We know that Puffer, but where after we get to the Faery World? Who do we look for?" Kegs asked.

"No. This time you *really* are going to Timbuktu, or

83

somewhere very near it at any rate. Ask Shimmer to give the whirlwind codeword that will bring you to a man called Leo. The last time I heard, he was travelling in the area of Timbuktu. You must tell him that you're looking for the Yellow of *'tibar'*." Puffer said all this in a slightly distracted way.

"Ah rats, head. I wish I was going again, Puffer," Atlas pleaded.

"I'm afraid that's not –" Puffer was interrupted as Cissy Hourihan arrived. "– I'm glad you could make it, Miss Hourihan. How is your snake?"

"Fine," she replied.

I wondered to myself whether snakes jumped or crawled out of their skins.

"Yo . . . yo . . . you missed some very great excitement yestergrey, Cissy," Jambo said quietly.

"Have you got *my* phone?" she said, in a demanding way, to Puffer, not seeming particularly interested in Jambo's account of our recovery of Orange.

"Here it is, head." Atlas handed the phone over and she almost snatched it from him.

"What were you doing with my phone?" she hissed like one of her snakes, as she inspected it.

Atlas explained that Puffer had given the phone to him so he could go with us to find Orange. Cissy didn't look altogether happy about this development and she immediately started checking the inbox for messages.

"Were you expecting something from someone, Miss Hourihan?" Puffer asked in a strange fashion. One of his wrinkles had moved to behind his left ear and was fluttering away like a worm on a hook.

Cissy's face reddened and she immediately stopped what she was doing. "What . . . oh no . . . I . . . I just wanted to check and see if a text message I sent to you yestergrey got through."

"None from you, head, but there were a few from

somebody called **F**. We guessed it was a wrong number and erased the messages," Atlas said while winking at me.

"*What* . . . you did what . . . oh . . . thanks," Cissy muttered as she put the phone in her pocket. She caught my puzzled look and stared back at me with a 'mind your own business' glare.

"What's *tibar*, Puffer?" Kegs asked.

"Gold dust."

"You mean like glitter!" Sheevra shrieked.

Puffer nodded. "It's the brightest yellow you can get because it is usually recovered from a river-bed and so is very washed and very pure."

"Oh my goodness! If you bring me back some of that, I won't say a word about our quest, I promise," Sheevra squeeked, her eyes opening like saucers.

"What about your duty to King and country, head? Didn't IL DOCE make you sign an oath or sumphink, when you joined the DSS?" Atlas said in a sarcastic voice. He was intrigued, as we all were and even Cissy pulled herself away from the message minder on her phone to listen to what was being said.

"My mother insisted on a special condition in my oath which allowed matters of personal appearance, such as a trip to the hairdresser or plastic surgeon, to override matters of national concern." Sheevra was dead serious like, when she said this.

Tricks, Atlas and even Puffer snorted.

I have to tell you, I almost, almost mind, admired the way she stood up for her convictions. Uniform or not, and unlike Cissy's snake, it would have been too much to expect that she'd have completely changed skins. Once a shaper, always a shaper like!

"I'm sure that is possible but you had better be going." Puffer was still wrinkling as he opened his orb watch and looked at the moving balls for a moment. "Are you ready, Mister Murphy?" He smiled at Kegs.

"Yeah. I'm mellow yellow, man. Let's go, lads!" Kegs shouted as he typed in 'Raincolour' on his phone and put his hand over Timbuktu. While he waited for us to the same, he had a fierce happy smile on his face. In fact he looked happier than I'd ever seen him before.

Kegs always saw the bright side in situations but, sometimes, I thought he did this to avoid any disappointment from hurting him. When he was very small, his real mum and dad had been killed in a train crash. This had happened after they had left him with his grandmother and were running away. They were very young and frightened. Kegs blamed himself for causing them to want to run away. After the funerals – one of the biggest ever seen in Dripsey, my mother said – Kegs was taken into care by the Department of Changing Families (DOCF) until they found a new family for him to live with.

Missus Murphy, who was also Kegs' aunt, and her husband adopted him. He worried now that Missus and Mister Murphy were fighting a lot and the same thing might happen all over again. He didn't like the crowd in the Department of Changing Families with their stiff smiles and all their questions about television abuse and where the beer barrels had come from.

"How can you answer a multiple choice questionnaire on choices, when you've got none?" he once asked me, after one of the visits from the stiff smilers of the DOCF. I think Kegs saw the chance to get the colour Yellow back as his way of making everything better again. Kegs was like that like. He always wanted to make things all right and as I put my hand over the others on the map he gave me a huge wink. The guy was in the groove like.

Kegs, Jambo, Tricks, Cissy and I waited for the tunnel to open up and this time it was definitely a lot less noisier.

The gate and schoolyard wall in the Faery World were also in heap of rubble but there the stones were hovering in the air and slotting themselves back into place like a jigsaw. The owl was directing the operation and would let out a terrible screech when any of the thick bricks got it wrong. When Cissy moved closer to watch what was going on, the owl screeched even louder, twisted its head round and round and flapped its wings like mad until Cissy backed off. She probably still smelt of snakes like, I thought, puzzled at the owl's reaction.

Strange thing, like, after all of our adventures so far and the things we'd seen, nothing surprised me anymore. It just seemed so normal like.

Shimmer was waiting for us. I thought she looked more and more beautiful every time I saw her. She smiled at me and I went bright red with embarrassment. I knew then that she was able to read my thoughts, like Puffer.

"You're getting used to all this now, Bull, are you not?" she said sweetly.

"I guess," I mumbled, mortified.

"Whom do you seek?"

"A man called Leo, but don't ask me what mood he's in," Kegs answered. "What's the password for the whirlwind, Shimmer?"

"The man you seek has only one mood and that is to keep moving. The password is 'Solomon's Mines'."

"How do you spell Solomon?" Kegs said shyly. He was a bit embarrassed like, as he pulled out his phone. Spellings and him, you need to understand, just didn't add up, if you catch my drift. The stiff smilers of the DOCF used to make a big deal about it.

"S . . . o . . . l . . . o . . ." Cissy called out each letter in a narky way.

"Go easy will ya! I've a slow brain," Kegs protested. If he had any shortcomings, pride wasn't one of them. He tapped in '♠□●□', in FDTL. Cissy completed the spelling and soon Kegs had added in the remaining letters; 'O□■♦ ♦)(■ℿ♦'.

"Solomon's Mines. There, I'm finished!" he said with some satisfaction.

"Bull. A word of caution." Shimmer walked towards me. She held out her hand.

"What is it?" I shouted over the noise of the rising wind. Her hand was warm and I squeezed it tightly.

"When a skeleton points, check his joints!" she shouted back.

At least that's what I thought she said as I was pulled away by the whirlwind wrapping around us.

The next thing we knew was that we were sitting at the edge of a river. It was very warm and a dense, hazy mist surrounded us. Out in the middle of the river we saw a man paddling a canoe. For a moment we thought it was a mirage but then he shouted over at us.

"How is it with you my fellow travellers?" He had a deep voice.

"Well, thank you. We are looking for a man called Leo," Kegs called out.

The man in the canoe changed directions and headed for us. After a bit of manoeuvring he landed and stood up to get out of the canoe. He was very tall and once again reminded me a bit of Puffer, as Bolus and Dainty Dante had also done. He was wearing a long, white, flowing robe, like a big shirt, with a belt in the middle into which a curved dagger was stuck. He had a bright yellow turban on his head.

"Hello, my friends," he said with a big smile as he brought his hand to his forehead in greeting. He was missing a few teeth.

"Wh . . . wh . . . who are you?" Jambo asked, returning the greeting.

"I am Leo Africanus, of course. The man you seek. I am a *Yuruk*, a nomad walker, a man who does not need to go anywhere but needs to be moving."

"Where are we?" I asked.

"Do you see the river?" He pointed up to where it came out of the mist.

"Yeah," we answered together.

"Away beyond the mist, perhaps fourteen days against the current in a canoe, is the river's beginning, is the land of Solimana where I have just come from."

"You mean Soloman's Mines?" Tricks asked.

"No. Solomon's Mines are a fable. There are no mines but Solimana is the mountainous area where the three great rivers of gold in Africa begin. This river in front of us is the Niger and it starts there, but so also do the Gambia and Senegal rivers."

"What do you mean by rivers of gold?" Cissy asked.

"The old geographers and mapmakers heard stories of a fabulous river in Africa, in which gold could be simply picked from the bed in big lumps. They thought that this was a single river of gold that stretched right across Africa, from the west to the east. It was only when travellers like me put them right that they realised it was a group of rivers which flowed in different directions but which all began in one spot – the mountains of Solimana."

"Are there people there?" Jambo asked.

"Yes. There are multitudes of men, women and children who working together like ants, spend their whole lives at the heads of the rivers collecting the gold dust that filters out in the water from the mountains. From there it goes all over the known world." Leo Africanus spread his hands out in a wide circle.

"You mean *tibar*?" Kegs said.

"Yes, *tibar*. The brightest Yellow of God's light."

"That's what we came here to find," Kegs said again.

"Why?" he asked.

We told him the whole story and he listened very carefully without interrupting.

"Can you help us like?" I asked.

"Perhaps. But it will be very dangerous."

"In wh . . . wh . . . what way, effendi?" Jambo looked worried, as if he suspected something bad.

"The people that work the rivers are not free. Their lives, are controlled by the slave traders working for the King of Mali, and they are forced to hand over the gold dust. The *tibar* is never held for long but is melted in the furnaces and made into lumps or ingots of gold metal. The colour changes in the heat and it is no longer bright yellow."

"How can we get some so, if it's all melted down?" Kegs asked.

"Every year some of the brightest and most yellow *tibar* is kept back and sent to the north as a precious present to the King of the Corsairs on the Barbary Coast, so that they can make a gold coin called the *sequin*. Until that journey is made the tibar is heavily guarded within the palace of Mansa Musa, the first King of Mali." Leo Africanus finished explaining and sat down on the bow of the boat.

"What are Corsairs?" I asked.

"Pirates. Murdering, child-killing pirates," Leo answered chillingly.

"Where is this palace of Mansa Musa?" Kegs asked.

"In the City of Skeletons, on the Island of the Jinn," Leo said quietly.

"The Island of the Jinn?" I asked in a seriously worried way. I'd had enough of islands of dead people when we went to get Orange. "Where's that like?"

"You are standing on it!" He replied with a flicker of his eyebrows.

"*Flaming Norah!*" I shouted, wanting to hop into the canoe and get the hell out of there like.

12

THE COLOUR YELLOW

✳〰ᛗ ᛗ□●□◆□ ✿ᛗ●●□◆

Part 2. The City of Skeletons

The mist soon disappeared as the midday sun and a warm wind burnt it away. We found ourselves sitting on a small headland that jutted out into the middle of a lake with a river heading off either side of us. There was very little in the way of trees and flowers and strangely there were no fishermen or other people around. In fact it was very, very quiet.

"You carry on, lads, there is something I want to do," Cissy said out of the blue.

"What?" Kegs asked.

"Not that it's any of your business but this looks like good snake territory. I want to have a look around. I'll be back soon," she answered as she wandered off.

She was probably just looking for snakes but we thought, at one point, we heard a phone ringing in the distance.

"You were going to tell us about the island, Leo?" Tricks said.

"This is the Island of the Jinn or Genies," Leo Africanus, the *Yuruk*, said as he stood up to his full height. "Many, many years ago Solomon, the great and wise king, got tired of all the evil spirits in the world and had them captured and bottled up in special jars and brought here. The King of Mali, Mansa Musa, built a special prison to keep them in but one by one over the years the jinn have escaped and caused great trouble. When the last one was finally free he placed a curse on the city of Mansa Musa."

"Wha . . . wha . . . what was the curse?" Jambo interrupted.

"For locking us in, lose your skin! Stay that way, for ever and a day!" Leo whispered as he paced up and down.

"Wicked trick," Tricks applauded.

"It came to pass. The king and all the people were turned into skeletons and have remained that way since. That's why nobody comes here, they are too afraid. It's a very safe place to hide the *tibar*."

"How do we get there?" Kegs asked. I admired his determination.

"I'll give you my compass and if you follow the needle due north, you will come upon the city." He gave the compass to Kegs.

"Are yo . . . yo . . . you not coming with us?" Jambo asked, a little worried like.

"No, my friends. I will meet you again in Timbuktu, which is on the far side of the river at the other end of the island. There are things I must attend to first in that city," Leo Africanus said quietly as he stepped into his boat and started to push off. He stopped suddenly and bent down to lift a package out of the canoe and throw it in my direction. "Use this, my friends for a trade."

"What is it?" I asked catching the package.

"Salt. Around here, they always need salt," he shouted back as the canoe was soon taken out of sight by the strong current.

"What's going on? Where's Leo gone?"

We turned to see Cissy walking towards us. She was smiling and in much better form.

"We're heading north to the City of Skeletons," I said, really cool like.

"Fine! Let's go." It didn't seem to faze her one bit and she just turned on her heel and started walking away again. Kegs rushed up to be alongside her with the compass.

Some four or five cowers later we came over the brow of a hill and there below us, smack in the middle of an oasis of palm trees, was a small city whose walls were made of mud. We didn't meet anybody when we reached the main gate so we started banging and banging.

"Open the gate," Kegs demanded.

"We're looking for King Mansa Musa," Tricks shouted.

Suddenly, the gate creaked open and ahead of us was a narrow street with the houses crowding in on both sides. There wasn't a sound in the place until we began to walk up the street. Our footsteps echoed off the windowless walls of the houses.

We were all a bit jittery when in the distance, at the far end of the street, we thought we could see some movement and we rushed to find out. The street opened up into a large square and in the middle of the square were ten girls dancing. We couldn't see anybody playing instruments but the music sounded like a chorus of randy cats. The dancing girls had veils, big, flowing trousers and pointy shoes on and we moved closer to get a better look. One of the girls stopped dancing, turned to face us and lifted her veil.

Now this was one of those moments when your heart stops and you want to pee.

She, the girl . . . it was a skeleton. A dancing skeleton, doing a bone dance instead of a belly wobble. I wished that Sheevra was there to see what all her dieting might lead too. A shiver went down my spine but she . . . it, the dancing skeleton, wagged a spidery finger and indicated for us to follow her.

"Wicked!" Tricks said as he looked everywhere for wires that might be controlling the skeletons.

We followed the bone-dancing skeleton down another dark

THE CITY OF SKELETONS

alleyway until we reached a dead end. There was a massive wall built of black, stone slabs, in the middle of which was a big set of doors made from pure gold. Miss Brittle, the name I'd given to the bone-dancer, pushed them open and we walked into a large hall. All around the hall, sitting and lying on chairs were more skeletons. Their jaws clattered open when they saw us and kept clattering until a voice spoke from the far end of the room.

"What do you want?" a ghostly voice speaking from the shadows asked. Ahead of us a weedy looking skeleton with a huge crown on his skull was sitting on a golden throne.

"We are looking for King Mansa Musa," Kegs said.

"Boney M even," Tricks added.

"Crawl and approach," the shadow voice demanded.

We looked at one another and nodded. Getting down on all fours we crawled towards the throne. Whenever we tried to look up a ruddy big bonecrusher skeleton poked us with a spear. "Keep your heads down, skin people." His had been the shadow voice.

"Sticks and stones might break my bones but words will never hurt me," Kegs said bravely. He got a dig of the spear for his trouble.

"I am King Mansa Musa. What do you seek here, people with skin?" the crowned skull asked from the throne.

"*Tibar*," Kegs mumbled nervously, with one eye on the spear of the bonecrusher. "Just a little mind."

"*Tibar*. That is a very precious commodity. What do you have to trade for it?" The crown had slipped over the king's skull so it hung like a necklace around where his neck should have been.

"Salt," I said loudly as I slid the package Leo had given me towards the throne. There was a lot of clattering in the room. They all seemed pleased.

"Very well, skin people. Go into the next hall and look for the signal of the silk merchant. He will lead you to the *tibar* you seek."

As King Mansa Musa clapped his hands together and one of his finger bones fell off and landed on the floor in front of my nose. The big bone-crushing spear-carrier picked it up and put

95

it carefully back in place on the king's hand before prodding us backwards out of the throne room and into another hall.

When we were able to get back up on our feet we could see that there were loads of skeletons standing, dead still like, in front of stalls that held every kind of exotic stuff you could think of. Stuff like lizard tongues, crocodile bags, elephant feet stools, dried dung balls and much, much more. None of the skeletons moved, so we began to look around.

"Over here. Quick!" Cissy shouted.

The rest of us rushed to the very far end of the room to where she was standing. There was a skeleton sitting on a small elephant footstool in front of a stall that had bundles and bundles of silk scarves. There was a sign over the stall that read,

Wazzim Boneapart Hassan
Silk Merchant.

As we looked at the stall the skeletons right arm suddenly shot out to point towards a small trapdoor that was tucked away on the far wall. If skeletons can smile, he had one, until I realised it was a small snake curling through the broken teeth of its jaw. Cissy picked up the snake and put it in her pocket.

"It's a very small door," Tricks said.

"You go ahead. I'm too tall so I'll stay here and watch," Cissy volunteered. She seemed very anxious for us to go on ahead.

"No. Bull, Tricks and I will go. Jambo will stay here with you," Kegs said in a very authoritative manner.

"Why?" Cissy demanded.

"Jambo has a big bottom and might get stuck. Anyway it's better if two of you stay together. This is my colour and my decision. Ok!" Kegs snapped. Cissy muttered.

It was a very, very small trapdoor and after pushing it open we squeezed through, one after another. Once through we found ourselves in a narrow tunnel, which was very dark and its floor sloped downwards and was very slippery. We started sliding and sliding and sliding.

Down and down through the tunnel we slid until we landed with a thud in the middle of a small room. It was full of equipment for tying people up and torturing them like in the sports gym at home. There were no windows and just one small candle flickering on a ledge near the ceiling.

We could hear the entrance trapdoor thumping closed behind us and then came the sound of running water. Only it wasn't water. The room began to fill up with sand and soon it was nearly up to our necks. We were shouting out. Nobody could hear us.

"Get on Bull's shoulders, Tricks. Use your phone to contact Jambo. Get him to use his wish. Hurry," Kegs ordered.

As Tricks climbed on my back the sand was going into my nostrils. His weight pushed me down further into the sand. I couldn't breath. I could hear that Kegs was also choking. I started to black out.

The next thing I knew, the three of us were in the hall again standing beside the still pointing skeleton of Wazzim Boneapart Hassan, the Silk Merchant. There was no sign of Jambo or Cissy. We started calling out their names and looking everywhere.

"Where have they gone? Jambo must have got the message and used his wish," Kegs was puzzled.

I was searching around the stall when I spotted the snake crawling around Wazzim's left hand. It was there and then that I spotted that it had the fingers of his hand crossed. I remembered Shimmer's warning. *When a skeleton points, check his joints.* The skeleton had tricked us. They weren't going to give us any *tibar*, if they could help it.

"What'll we do now?" Kegs coughed out some sand as he spoke. "We're no nearer to Yellow!"

"We'll have to find Jambo and Cissy first. Their phones are

not responding and I can't get through to Puffer either," Tricks said in a worried voice as he shook sand from his phone.

Ours were the same.

"We can't even call up the whirlwind," Kegs added.

"Let's get to Timbuktu and ask Leo for help," I suggested.

The others agreed and we walked back out through the market hall and crept into the main palace hall to make for the door. Just when we thought we could get away quietly, we came in for a very rude shock like.

King Mansa Musa suddenly spotted us from the far end of the room and he started going to pieces with anger. We couldn't make out what he was shouting but very soon, some seriously big brutes of skeletons came chasing out after us from the shadows. They all had an ugly jawbone grin, really white pointed teeth and very long, sharp nails that Sheevra would have been proud of.

"Get them, my Keres. Get them! Return the skin people to our shadows !" Mansa Musa was shouting.

"Rattle and run, lads," Tricks shouted as the Keres flapped their red cloaks and seemed to fly towards us.

They were screeching a horrible screech, like a pig squealing and we didn't hang around. We ran like mad, dodging the Keres in and out of dark alleyways all the way through the city. We hadn't a clue where we were going and suddenly ran into a dead end. There was a large archway at the end of the alleyway that led into a dark tunnel from which we could hear the sound of a waterfall. When we turned to see where the Keres were we nearly wet ourselves. They were right in our faces like and their nails were beginning to scratch at the air.

"In here," I shouted as I ducked under the archway and into the tunnel. Kegs and Tricks followed but the Keres didn't.

13

THE COLOUR YELLOW

✳〰Ⅲ Ⅲ□●□◆□ ✿Ⅲ●●□◆

Part 3. Timbuktu and Tosee the Ferryman

As we walked further and further down the tunnel the noise of rushing water got louder and louder. We finally reached a riverbank, where two canoes were tied up. One looked very old and battered and there was water leaking in through a large hole in the side. Sitting in the other canoe was a hunched figure, covered in a dirty brown cloak like a monk. The hood of the cloak was so large that we couldn't see whether he was a skeleton or not but unlike the others back in the palace he did seem to have eyeballs. There were two red spots deep in the hood, which moved to follow our movements and also reflected the light from a small fire that was in a brazier beside the canoe. He didn't seem all that surprised about our sudden arrival, it was as if he was expecting us.

"Who are you?" Kegs asked.

"My name is Tosee. I'm the guardian of the gate into the City of Skeletons," the hooded figure cackled.

"But we didn't see you when we came to the city," Kegs said disbelievingly. "The gate was open and we walked right in."

"That is the old gate. Nobody enters the city any more by that way. You were the first in a long, long time. Now you have to come on the underground river to here. I am also the ferryman, see, so I should know. I am responsible for transporting people to the City of Skeletons on the Island of the Jinn."

"Can you bring us to the other side?" I asked. "We need to get to Timbuktu."

"No. I'm afraid not," the ferryman, Tosee answered. "I only take people whose lives are looking in this direction. If you want to take my canoe it may only be for a short journey out to drink the 'water of forgetfulness' from the middle of the river and then you have to come back again to here. You'll have to take the other canoe if you wish to leave the island."

"But it's rotten!" Kegs said. "We'll sink?" He would have given anything then for Norah's Flotation Device.

"Then it appears you do not have any choice. You are right. The nine currents of the river will sink you and you will drown. Why not just stay and become skeletons. The Keres who are waiting for you in the alleyway will have your skin off in a flash. There will be no . . . well, not much pain. It's often hard to be sure with young ones," he cackled again. "Why go the the bother of drowning first?"

"Did you say your boat can only carry people who are looking in this direction?" Tricks asked suddenly.

"Yes!" Tosee answered.

"Lads, I've an idea," Tricks, the riddle-man whispered in our ears and we smiled.

"We will take up your offer of a place in your canoe." Kegs puffed his chest out as he said this.

"Very well. It will be a very short journey so. Hop in."

We got in and stood up in the boat and looked back at Tosee as he pushed off. As the canoe got further and further away from the riverbank it got more and more difficult to see anything. Thankfully, the small fire, which Tosee had been using to warm his bones was still flickering. We kept looking at that.

"We are now in the middle. Why not look at the river and

then drink some of its water," Tosee asked in a pleasant voice.

"No! We are only going to look in one direction. You must keep paddling until we turn or look away," Kegs said.

"You have tricked me!" Tosee screeched angrily.

"Too right, bonehead," Tricks said. He had guessed right again. By looking in the direction of the tunnel leading to the City of Skeletons we appeared to want to go there. Tosee, was obliged to keep paddling.

After a while, we could see by the brightness that the underground river was coming up into the light. Our shadows were falling towards Tosee.

"Were nearly there, lads! Don't turn now!" Tricks shouted.

Suddenly from behind me a phone rang. I was nearest to the bow and it was somewhere close. I began to turn. Tosee was laughing.

"Stop, Mister Sheehan. Don't turn until the boat reaches land." It was Leo Africanus's voice. He was very close and as the canoe bumped against something soft I felt two hands hauling me out quickly. Kegs and Tricks followed soon after. Tosee, had pulled his hood right over, as if his eyes were being hurt by the light. He was crying.

"*Flaming Norah!* That was close," I said to the others.

"Pay the ferryman Mister Sheehan, otherwise he will wait there for you for ever," Leo Africanus said in a serious voice.

'With what?" I asked.

"Here's some more salt. He'll take that." Leo gave me a small packet and I threw it towards Tosee. At the very moment his boney but skin-covered hand grabbed it out of the air the phone I heard earlier rang again. I rushed to the canoe and found Cissy's phone on the bottom hidden by a coil of rope. I grabbed the phone and pushed the canoe away from the shore. Tosee was cursing us.

"How did that get there?" Kegs asked.

"Cissy must have dropped it when she was taken by the

ferryman. I wonder if she used the same trick as us or is she already a skeleton," Tricks mumbled.

"No, she is not," Leo Africanus said, "She and your other friend Jambo were taken by the slave traders and put on display in the slave market. Both of them were bought by a man working for Redbeard, the King of the Corsairs."

"Where are they now?" I asked.

"They leave tomorrow, with the camel train carrying the *tibar* to the north. They are being held at the hotel of the caravan drivers near the end of the town.

"We'll have to sneak in and free them?" Kegs said.

"Yeah and try and get the *tibar* as well!" Tricks added.

"Can you help us Leo?" I asked.

Leo Africanus flashed his teeth and smiled. "I already have a cunning plan but it will present a severe test of your bravery."

"My middle name!" Tricks said.

"Severe?" I teased.

"No, 'bravery', you turd." Tricks tried giving me a kick.

"Stop messing you two!" Kegs demanded, "We must get organised. Tell us your plan, Leo."

Leo took out an orb-watch, which was very like Puffer's one, except there were only seven balls instead of the ten in Puffers. He looked at me.

"You are observant young man. In my time we only know of the seven planets we can see with our own eyes, the Sun, the Moon, Saturn, Mars, Mercury, Jupiter and Venus. There are some eyeglasses, telescopes I think you call them, but they are not very good. It doesn't matter however, I can get more than enough information from the planets that I do have and it is very interesting." Leo smiled.

"In what way?" Kegs asked.

"Tonight . . ." He held up the orb-watch to look carefully at it. ". . . yes, definitely tonight, there is going to be a lunar eclipse. That will provide the opportunity."

"What do you mean by a lunar eclipse?" Tricks asked.

"The earth, on which we are standing will get in the way of the sunlight, from the dark side, shining on the moon. For about twenty minutes the moon will be blacked out," Leo explained.

"How will that help us?" I wondered.

"Ah . . . that is the beauty of it! In the religion of Islam, everybody has to perform five daily prayers but there are some unusual occasions when they *must* say other prayers. One is when there is an eclipse of the sun by the moon and the other when there is an eclipse of the moon by the earth. Tonight when the eclipse of the moon happens, all the camel drivers and the guards will have to go to prayer. It will be your only chance and you must move fast." Leo Africanus closed his watch.

It was much later when we sneaked through the town and made our way to the big Caravan Hotel on the outskirts. Now this hotel like, was a bit of a dive. Camels and men were asleep on the ground together and it was hard to figure out who was snoring the loudest or who smelt the worse. There was still a full moon and we must have looked like ghosts tiptoeing our way to the spot where Leo had figured Redbeard's camels would be kept.

It was easy in the end because all the camels had a skull-and-crossbones mark branded onto their butts and there were guards with huge swords patrolling around the camels. In one corner, three baskets were together and there was another guard, bigger than all the others, watching over these. He was one ugly dude, with a big turban and an earring in one ear. He was chewing something and kept trying to kill the loads of flies in the yard with his spit.

"That must be the *tibar*," I whispered, pointing to the baskets from our hiding place behind a load of camel dung.

We kept watching the sky, and sure enough, as Leo had predicted we could see a black, curved shadow moving across the moon. After a few minutes the moon disappeared altogether and all the guards started running about and waking up the camel drivers. They seemed a bit frightened to me, and were fierce excited. There was a mosque or church beside the hotel and soon the yard was deserted as they went into pray. The big brute guarding the baskets didn't move but knelt down on a basket near them.

"Now's your chance," Leo Africanus said. "Put some of this in all of their water flasks." He held out a bottle to each of us. "When they finish praying they will take a drink before going back to sleep."

"What is it?" Tricks asked.

"The 'water of forgetfulness' from the middle of the underground river. It will knock them out," Leo answered.

We took a bottle each and ran around the camp putting a few drops into each water flask we found. Kegs had to get the guard's one but he managed, without the big fellow noticing. Once finished we ran back to where we were hiding and waited.

The eclipse passed and all the people left the mosque. As Leo had predicted they all took a drink from their bottles and soon were conked out asleep.

"What will we do now?" Tricks asked.

"Ring Jambo's phone," I said. "When we hear it ringing we will know where he is."

I did this and nothing happened. Not a peep, like.

"Let's go for the *tibar* and get some of that anyway." Kegs, was not to be distracted from his mission.

We nodded and crept over to where the big guard was fast asleep. A hand was draped over a basket.

"Open the lid," Kegs whispered.

"*Flaming Norah!*" I shouted out before Tricks covered my mouth. Jambo was in the basket looking up at us. One of the other baskets began to rock and when we took off the lid there was Cissy. Both Cissy and Jambo's hands and feet were tied and they had a dirty rag stuffed in their mouths. We hauled them out of the baskets and began to untie them.

"I have it, I have it," Kegs shouted. He had lifted the lid of the third basket. As we looked over at him, his face was lit up by the brightest yellow light I'd ever seen. *"Whoooopeeee!"* he shouted.

"Shhhhhhhhhhh," Tricks hissed.

Too late! The guard started moving. The water was wearing off fast. First one eye opened and then the other. His hand went for his sword. He let out a huge roar.

"There are thieves at the **tibar***. To arms!"*

TIBAR CARAVAN
LEAVING THE
CITY OF SKELETONS

"Fill your pockets quick, Kegs and let's get the hell out of here like," I shouted.

While Kegs dug in his hands, I called up the whirlwind on my phone by texting in '◆□●□○□■⊠◆ ◆⁂⊁■Պ◆'. The wind started rising, spewing a dust storm all over the yard. The guards, drivers and camels were coughing. We ran from the yard and holding hands went into the middle of it.

Shimmer was waiting for us. She seemed anxious. We had been gone a long time, even for the Faery World.

"Hurry, hurry," she said urgently. "Mister Malone's mother is walking up the pathway to the school."

Kegs tapped in **'Raincolour'** and after putting our hands on Timbuktu we were soon back in the school. Atlas and Sheevra were waiting. Puffer Penhaligan was nowhere to be seen. Mister Penhaligan was talking to Kegs' mother in the schoolyard. She looked angry.

"Where were yous, heads? You've been gone for hours," Atlas asked, a bit worried like.

"Did you get it?" Sheevra asked.

Kegs smiled as he emptied his pockets of the yellow *tibar* into an old marmalade bottle we used for catching wasps in the school. We had to stop Sheevra from grabbing it but she still managed to get some.

At that moment Missus Murphy marched into the room and up to Kegs. She pulled him out by the ear.

"Where were you, Alphonus Murphy? You should have been home ages ago? The people from the Department of the Changing Families are waiting in the house for you," she nagged at him.

Kegs looked back at us as he was dragged out and gave us a huge wink.

'Alphonus', I thought to myself, trying not to laugh. No wonder he never told us his first name.

14

THE COLOUR GREEN

⁑〰ᛗ ᛗ□●□◆□ ⅃□ᛗᛗ■

Part 1. MacUbartutu

The following morning Tricks and I made our way up the main street to the school together. There were some workmen busy taking down all the old street-name signs and putting up new ones instead. From now on the main road into and out of Dripsey was to be called the Devine Way. Apart from this activity, the town was fierce quiet with Chameleon tanks, like Missus Devine's, and some military policemen from the Army controlling the two roads into the town. Tricks asked one of the army fellahs why they were there and he said they had been told to put Dripsey in quarantine because of the PANDA virus and nobody was to be left in or out, without good reason like. He also said that the same thing was happening to towns all over the country to stop people who had gone off their wick from the loss of colour from causing any more trouble.

There was no sign of Sergeant Ulysses Finnegan at the crossroads but some of the big girls from the secondary school, who were members of IL DOCE Devine's Shadowtime Soldiers, were patrolling the streets. Tricks was dead keen like, to go up to the DSS girls and get their telephone numbers to put in his phone, but when he tried, against my advice like, they mostly ignored him and even threatened to put him in jail if he annoyed them anymore. The dude was devastated, psychologically scarred even.

There were also rumours that Norah O'Toole was already in jail for disturbing the peace, when the CATA (Coalition Against Television Abuse) protestors tried to cut the power lines into the town. One of the big DSS girls, a girl Tricks really fancied, shouted after us that Kegs and Mister Murphy had been arrested for trying to break Norah out of the lockup. She also took enormous pleasure in telling us that Kegs had been taken to the Happy Gulag detention centre, set up by the stiff smilers from the Department of Changing Families, where he was probably now being tortured with more multiple-choice questions.

Speaking of televisions, IL DOCE had announced, on Sky and Sea News, that because of all the riots around the country he was suspending the government and that new elections were not going to be held. He went on to say that under the emergency powers available to him he had taken over the running of the country, would be selecting a date for his coronation as King, and that from now on the television stations would only be showing interior-decorating programmes like 'Changing Shades'. He also announced that he planned to marry Katie Allteeth, the reporter from S&S News, and make her his Queen.

When we got to the school, Puffer, Atlas, Cissy and Jambo were waiting for us.

"Did you hear about Kegs, head?" Atlas asked.

"Yeah, but he'll pull the wool over their eyes," I answered, fairly sure that he would. "He's getting the hang of those MCQ's by now."

"From what Miss Hourihan and Mister Kitangiri have been telling me, Mister Murphy was quite a hero," Puffer said as he picked up the jam-jar of *tibar* to look at it.

"Yeah, Alphonus 'Kegs' Murphy is the right stuff alright. He was brilliant, like, and we. . ." I stopped speaking when I saw Cissy Hourihan scoffing a bit. That really browned me off.

108

There were some things that happened in the City of the Skeletons that I didn't understand and that I wanted to ask her about. ". . . what happened, Cissy, to you and Jambo, after we went into the trapdoor and there's something else as well . . . your phone keeps picking up wrong numbers. What's going on?" All the thoughts came racing out of my mouth like.

"The slave traders arrived in the hall as we were waiting for you and it was they that pulled the hidden lever to let in the sand." Cissy was being a bit defensive like, as she answered.

"Yes. That is true. We . . . we . . . just got your message as they carried us off t . . . t . . . to the boat. I ha . . . had to turn it off after making ma . . . ma . . . my wish," Jambo agreed.

"And what about the messages to Cissy's phone?" I persisted.

"I'm sorry, Mister Sheehan, but we will have to seek that information at another time. As you have seen, things are getting out of hand here in Dripsey and we still have four colours to get. You should get moving," Puffer interrupted, to Cissy's relief.

"Hoo . . . hoo . . . who do I ask for?" Jambo asked.

"Ask Shimmer to direct you to a man called **MacUbartutu**," Puffer replied.

"Where's Sheevra?" Tricks asked.

"We won't see her for dust, head, if you know what I mean. Her mum's tank has gone in for a service and to have the water cannon changed to a gun that fires sidewinder missiles. Sheevra is supervising the installation of mirrors so she can keep an eye on herself as well as everyone else." Atlas shook his head as he said this.

"Has she said anything about the quest?" I asked Puffer.

"Not as far as I know, but power can corrupt." A couple of wrinkles swapped places in a sad way. "Now . . . you really must get going. Mister Kitangiri, please put in the password." Puffer's wrinkles seemed very anxious.

Jambo took out his phone and began to tap in the code. Suddenly he stopped.

"I . . . I . . . am afraid." he said looking down at the ground. His hands were shaking. "I . . . am very afraid."

I think the run in with the slave traders had upset Jambo terribly. He came from a part of Africa where for many hundreds of fears people had been taken by others to be slaves and were never seen again. His own family had to leave Africa more recently because they were being chased, not by the government or by soldiers or slavers, but by what he told us was a fight between good and evil spirits in the town where he lived. The evil spirits like, were known as the Cat Brothers and wanted Jambo to become the 'Lionman of Singida' (Whisper this name or better still don't say it at all! – Jambo's instructions.) and were going to snatch him away from his family.

The Lionman of Singida, he told us, was a young boy whom the Cat Brothers would pick on when he was our age and then lock up in a room for ten fears. In that time the boy would be brainwashed and would be slowly changed into a lion. Eventually a grey would come when the evil spirits would open the door and let the Lionman free to start doing their dirty work for them, like killing animals and people and running governments.

Atlas said that it was probably like being whisked off to one of the boys' secondary schools in the city. 'Academies for crack heads', his older brother had called them, and he would know, as he had been to most of them at one time or another.

I guessed like, that Jambo's family had run away from the evil spirited Cat Brothers in his town because Jambo was a pussycat and not a lion.

"It is normal, Mister Kitangiri but that fear will make you careful. If you are careful then you will be safe." Puffer touched Jambo gently on the shoulder. "Green is your responsibility and I know that you will not fail."

Jambo smiled weakly, as if only half believing him, and typed in **'Raincolour'** before putting his hand on Timbuktu. The spot on the map was getting quite worn.

"Best of luck, heads." Atlas waved as he left the room.

"Where are you off to?" I called after him.

"To rescue Kegs from his multiple choice torture. I know a secret way in to the Happy Gulag. See ya, heads." He was gone.

One by one Tricks, Cissy and I put our hands over Jambo's and soon the tunnel opened up. It was a well-oiled machine by now and there was only a gentle whirring noise as we entered.

Shimmer was waiting and I found my face getting red when I saw her again. She looked sad.

"Hello my friends," she said quietly.

"What's wrong, Shimmer?" I asked.

"My screech-owl is missing. He's never done that before." She sounded really worried.

I have to tell you that I wanted to use my wish there and then to get her owl back but, reading my thoughts, Shimmer looked at me and shook her head.

"We'll keep an eye out for it," Tricks said, trying to be helpful.

Cissy didn't seem bothered at all, like. So much for her liking animals I thought, but then remembered that the owl didn't much like Cissy either.

"Thank you, my friends, that is very kind of you. Now who are you looking for this time?" she said sweetly.

"Ma . . . ma . . . MacUbartutu." Jambo answered.

"Wow! That is a very far off mood my friends. The codeword for the whirlwind is 'Shuruppak'." Shimmer looked up towards the sky as Jambo typed in '◆≋◆□◆□□☺&' before turning to whisper in my ear, *"Bull, be careful not to turn your back on the Stone Ones!"*

The whirlwind formed and it seemed a lot longer than usual

before we found ourselves coming out into the middle of a valley of the brightest flowers and greenest grass you've ever seen. Ahead of us was a pond, which had a large fountain in it and was full of big goldfish and all around us stretching up to the sky were high cliffs with pictures of men and chariots carved into the stone of the rocks.

There were one or two of these pictures that really caught my eye. One was of a huge eagle with its wings spread out and looking down on a geezer with a high hat and another was of two winged men holding a tree. Not far off from the pond was a round tower on the top of which a fire was burning in a big pot.

"Where are we, I wonder?" Tricks asked when his head stopped spinning.

"We'll soon find out," Cissy replied as she pointed to a man and woman who were coming towards us in a chariot, that was being pulled by two enormous white buffalos. There were also two dogs running alongside the chariot.

The man who held the reins of the buffalo was as tall as Puffer, but the weirdest thing like, his face was just like a baby's, with big red cheeks and eyes and yet he had grey hair like Puffer's that trailed out behind the chariot, like you see behind girls in fancy weddings. The woman with him was big and plump and had a lovely warm smile.

"Where are we?" I shouted.

"The Fields of Paradise, my young friends," he answered back.

"We . . . we . . . we're looking for MacUbartutu," Jambo called out as they came close.

"Why?" The man asked.

"We are looking for the colour Green," Cissy snapped.

"I'm no wiser," he said, looking at me.

I then told him our story, in my own way like. When I finished there was a long silence when he said nothing. We just

112

sat there for ages like gombeens, our mouths behaving like the stupid goldfish in the pond, before he spoke again.

"That is a dangerous quest, my friends, a very dangerous quest indeed! The 'Green' you seek is the *'plant of the heartbeat'*. It holds the secret of living forever, if you eat its powers. Look around you!" He pointed up at the carvings on the cliff. "Gilgamesh and other braver people than you have looked for it before and failed. Why should you find it?" the man said haughtily.

"Be . . . be . . . because we don't want it for ourselves, it is for others," Jambo suddenly growled like a lion, and not a pussycat.

The baby-faced man's eyes opened wider and he smiled at Jambo. "That is a very good answer, my brave young warrior. I am MacUbartutu, and this is my wife," he said, pointing to the jolly woman beside him. I thought she was his mother like. "Some call me the distant mood, but I am no further or no closer than you think. The Green colour you seek is the colour of a coral plant which is only found deep in the 'Water of Life' far away from here. You will have to travel along the black river and then the white Star Path to retrieve it." He pointed towards the west.

"How far?" I asked, knowing we couldn't use the whirlwind. I didn't much like the sound of the scorpions either like.

"You must follow the sun and go to where it goes. When it catches up with you from behind look for the start of the Star Path. Choose the path that brings you closest to the tail of the snake and the head of the dragon This will lead you through the guardian gates to the land of a thousand lakes. Be very careful though, because all of these lakes, save one, are known as the 'Waters of Death' and if you step in them or drink their waters you will perish. When you have found the right one, the 'Water of Life', you must dive beneath the waters to pluck the coral plant from the bottom. That plant is the source of all wisdom and all sadness. Be careful what you do with it." MacUbartutu looked at Cissy when he said this last sentence.

"How will we know which is the right lake?" she asked.

"Take this with you." MacUbartutu stepped down from the chariot and walked to the side of the pond. With a quick whip of his hand he plunged it into the pond and pulled out a goldfish. The poor fish's mouth opened and closed and its body flapped about for a few minutes before it went quite. He handed the fish to Jambo, who just looked at it, wondering whether he was expected to eat it or something.

"Wh . . . wh . . . what do I do with this?" Jambo said cautiously.

"Take the fish with you and holding its tail place it carefully on the surface of the lakes you find. When you reach the 'Water of Life' the fish will revive and live again. In that way you'll know." MacUbartutu got back up into the chariot again and began to urge the buffalo to turn.

"I still don't understand about the sun catching up with us from behind like," I said.

MacUbartutu took an orb-watch from his pocket and handed it down to me. It was like Puffer's and Leo Africanus' from the outside but when you opened it there was just a flat disc with two small, glass, crystal sticks standing up at either end like needles.

"It's a rainbow time dial," MacUbartutu explained, "Hold it up to the sun!"

When I did, the sun hit the crystal sticks and the light spread into all colours of the rainbow, which then went off in different directions. I looked carefully at the orb but still did not understand.

"Very nice, but how do we use it?" I asked shrugging my shoulders.

"When you get to the edge of the world, the sun will be in

front of you as well as behind. Hold the orb up and the light from both suns will create a different rainbow from each crystal at opposite ends of the dial. At an exact moment the different rainbows will come together on the dial and cancel each other out and there will be a black spot in the centre. When that happens you are very close to your journey's end and begining." MacUbartutu whistled and the buffalo began to move. "It will also lead you to the 'Water of Life' when you are amongst the lakes."

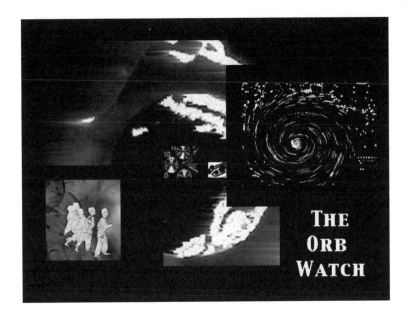

THE ORB WATCH

"Why not send Khiddir with them, husband?" The plump woman spoke.

"Who's Khiddir?" Cissy asked suspiciously.

"Khiddir is the keeper of the fishpond and the only person who knows how to spot the right coral plant when you reach the lake of the Waters of Life." MacUbartutu nodded in agreement with his wife. "He will help you."

"Take this to hold the heart." Missus MacUbartutu handed down a glass bottle to Jambo. I thought of the Golem again.

"Where is this, Khiddir dude?" Tricks asked. I could see he was thinking they might have a lot in common.

"Right behind you," MacUbartutu said as the chariot pulled away.

We all turned to see a fellow behind us making a daisy chain with the flowers. He looked exactly like Tricks in fact, his twin you could say . . . well, almost like, if you ignored the fact that your man, Khiddir, was green. Green eyes, green hair, green teeth, the lot. He even wore a green tracksuit with what looked like the Greenpeace logo on it.

"*Flaming Norah!*" I shouted as I nearly fell back into the pool.

"Wicked!" Tricks laughed. "Isn't he fierce handsome. I'm green with envy."

"No improvement!" Cissy said, almost funnily.

"Hoo . . . hoo . . . who is kidding hoo . . . who?" Jambo mumbled with a deadpan expression while looking at the dead fish in his hand.

15

THE COLOUR GREEN

❋〰ℳ ℳ□●□◆□ ♪□ℳℳ■

Part 2. Khiddir and the Scorpio Path

The green guy, Khiddir brought us to a river which flowed through the 'Fields of Paradise'. We very soon found out why he was called what he was called as he spoke in riddles every time we asked him a question.

Unlike normal rivers this one was not full of water but was made of black oil and once on board a raft made of marsh reeds we went with the flow towards the west. We had an escort of alligators, pretending to be dolphins, stay with us all the way like police motorcycle outriders and instead of seagulls there were black ravens following the raft. Because the river flowed west, the sun was directly ahead of us all the time but sinking lower and lower towards the ground. Every now and then like, I would turn around to see if there was a sun behind us as well.

The valley soon got narrower and narrower and the river headed for a narrow gap in the cliffs that surrounded the valley. It was a twisty dark gorge and all we could hear was the echoes of the sounds of the river coming back from the walls.

"We are very close to the edge of the world. . ." Khiddir finally spoke, as the raft suddenly burst into the sunshine after a long time travelling through the cliffs. ". . . and the place of the two lights."

"Wh . . . wh . . . what do we do now?" Jambo asked.

"It's in your power to capture light, the beginning then will be in sight!" Khiddir replied.

"What?" I said.

"He means the orb-disc, Bull." Tricks, blew on his fingers as he figured it out.

I held out the orb and its covers opened out like a flower. Ahead of us the sun was just dropping towards the horizon and the whole sky was a bright red-purple colour. Thousands of brightly coloured parrots were flying in all directions and the whole sky seemed alive. To either side of the river was a huge forest whose trees towered up towards the sky.

"Wh . . . wh . . . where is this?" Jambo asked as he looked at the trees whose branches, covered in moss, dipped into the river with the weight and whose roots were like fingers coming out to meet us.

"Where wet trees, brings birds and bees. Somewhere in the deep, are the lakes we seek. By the light of day, you'll find the way," Khiddir answered, in a manner of speaking, as he scanned the river-banks for a landing spot to guide the raft to.

"*Look!* Look behind us," Cissy suddenly shouted.

We all turned. We could still just see the narrow gap where the river of oil, we were travelling on, had come out from the valley through the high cliffs. Directly above the gap there was a huge picture carving of the sun on the cliff face. The white marble of the cliff was shining like a massive polished mirror. As the sun sank towards the horizon ahead of us, its reflection travelled up the river and after hitting the bottom of the cliff rose higher and higher up the cliff face until it reached the carving on the wall. When the sun's reflection hit the centre of the sun carving, a beam of light suddenly shot towards the raft.

"Look now with the crystals and let them speak, it is not a time for the frightened meek," Khiddir ordered.

I held up the orb-dial to try and catch the beams of light coming from both directions. First the light from the real sun ahead of us hit one crystal and split into a rainbow and then, the light from the reflection off the cliff hit the other and split into another rainbow. Both of these rainbows darted about all over the place for a while like, colouring our faces with oranges and yellows and greens and purples, before suddenly meeting in the middle.

After that it was like the light suddenly went out like. Where the two rainbows had been there was now a black ball that hovered above the centre of the dial, as if held by an invisible string joining the two crystal needles.

"*Flaming Norah!*" I gasped.

"Wicked!" Tricks said.

"Wo . . . wo . . . wonderful," Jambo added.

"What now?" Cissy asked, unamazed like.

"*We stop here without fear,*" Khiddir said confidently, as he looked towards the river-bank and pointed to a small clearing in the forest just ahead of us.

We all paddled like mad as he steered the raft towards the bank. When we got out we found that the small clearing was surrounded by dense wall of trees through which there were five different paths from which to choose. Each of the paths was marked by a rock that had had dots and lines carved on it. It was obviously a code but we hadn't an iota what type. *(See drawing at back of book.)*

"Wh . . . wh . . . which one?" Jambo asked.

"*I don't know yet I rejoice. It's your destiny and thus your choice,*" Khiddir said.

"What? You're meant to know the way," Cissy barked.

"Stop kidding, Khiddir," Tricks said.

"I think it would be easier all round if you stopped speaking in riddles. We understand that you are only a guide and you cannot make decisions for us but we don't have a huge amount of time. Are you definitely saying that you don't know the right path to take?" Cissy spoke again, impatiently.

119

"*Riddles come and riddles go, but for my fun it's all I know.*
But, very well, I will stop my riddles to save time, but I do not
lie about knowing which path, my friends," Khiddir said quietly
before looking at Cissy. "You are right, the path to discovering
the 'Water of Life" is different for everybody and you will now
have to wait until darkness to know which one to take." He
paused to stare up at the sky. "It will not be long, however. The
sun is nearly gone below the edge."

We waited there for about a cower and Tricks and Khiddir
spent the time exchanging jokes and trying to guess each other's
riddles. Every now and then one of them burst out laughing
which would disturb the fruit bats that were darting through
the trees. Cissy had gone down one of the paths to go for a pee,
she said, as if I was going to argue with her like and Jambo just
sat quietly, looking worried.

As it got darker and darker, fire flies were sparking all over
the place, and big, well-oiled, blinking, yellow alligator eyes
looked at us hungrily from the river. Deeper in the forest I swore
I heard whispering sounds and the hairs on the back of my neck
prickled as I stood up to investigate.

"Look up there, Bull, look at all the stars." My heart nearly
stopped as a voice suddenly spoke from behind me.

"*Fecking hell*, Cissy, don't sneak up on people like that . . .
wow!" I was stopped in my tracks by what I saw. The sky was
by now pitch black and all the stars had come on like magical
twinkling lights.

"Do you see the sky path of the winter geese?" Khiddir,
pointed upwards as he spoke.

"Yu . . . yu . . . you mean the Milky Way?" Jambo said with
a degree of astronomical certainty.

"Yes. The road of many stars that stretches across the night
sky and which the migrating geese use to find their way. It will
now show us the way as well." Khiddir looked at me.

"What do you mean?" I asked, puzzled like.

"Do you know anything about your Zodiac signs and the stars they were named after?" Khiddir asked.

"You mean horror scopes and things like that? My mum and sister read them every grey to figure out their numbers for the lottery," I said.

"It's *horoscopes* you moron," Cissy spat at me before turning to Khiddir. "Yes. Of course I do. It's basic stuff," she answered him in her most superior fashion.

The rest of us hadn't really a clue like, although we did occasionally read what our horror scopes had to say. I thought that they were a right load of cobblers most of the time, like for instance on the grey I was due to meet Tulips in the forest, they promised a liberating experience whereas I got clamped.

"Well, it was our people who were the first to chart the movement of the stars through the night sky. We use them to tell the season of planting from the season of harvesting and the destiny of our lives. What season is it in your world at present?" Khiddir asked no one in particular.

"The sixth lunth in the Year of the Fear. June in the old language," I said.

"I understand what you mean. The sixth moon cycle in our language is called *Kinninni*. Now listen carefully. You know that earth is now divided in 90 lines of separation from its middle, the Equator, to the top, the North Pole and also from the Equator to the South Pole. You come from a place near Line 52 North but where we are standing now is on Line 30 North. Are you following me?" He looked at all of us in turn.

"Line by line, dude." Tricks laughed.

"Think of the night sky as standing under an umbrella shade and we are facing towards the south. If we look up and slightly behind us you will see, almost directly above us, the polar star. Do you see?" We followed his pointing hand as he spoke.

"Ye . . . yes," Jambo said.

"Well, if you look forwards again you can see coming from in front and winding its way round the left side of the sky, the Milky Way, as you call it. That is the Star Path we have to follow. Do you see?" We nodded. "Now, if you imagine you are holding the umbrella and you are looking at its rim you can see, starting on the right side of the sky, the group of stars called Leo, then moving along the rim of the umbrella the groups of Virgo, Libra, Scorpio and Sagittarius in turn. These are five of the possible gateways to the heavens and your destiny but only two of these gates at this season of the year are within the path of the Milky Way. Look up and tell me which ones."

"Scorpio, the scorpion and Sagittarius, the archer," Cissy said with absolute conviction and, it has to be mentioned, without looking up.

"Yes, you are right. Although there are two gates within the Star Path you have to chose just one to follow. Only one path will bring you to the lakes." Khiddir held his hands out apologetically as he said this.

"Of course! The rocks marking the paths with all the dots and squiggles carved on them! I understand now! Each of th . . . th . . . the five paths from th . . . the clearing represents one of those star groups," Jambo said.

"Yes." Khiddir nodded.

"And the drawings on the signpost rocks are the star maps of those gates, to tell one from another," Tricks said.

"Yes, exactly. There are five paths from the clearing and each have a meaning, the Path of Strength the Path of Purity, the Path of Justice, the Path of Stealth and the Path of Accuracy. Each path is marked by a rock but not necessarily in sequence as the paths might start one way but then cross over, as in your lives. Luckily, you only have to choose one of two. Stealth or Accuracy."

"So which do we choose, Scorpio or Sagittarius?" I asked excitedly, thinking Khiddir already knew like. Like hell he did, he just shrugged his shoulders.

"It's Sagittarius," Cissy said loudly, in such a way as to end any arguments. "We should go that way."

"How do you know?" Tricks asked. He wasn't going to be bossed around by her either.

"F tol . . . a feeling tells me." Cissy hesitated when she said this.

"You don't have any feelings, girl," I snapped at her. I couldn't understand why I was so peed off with Cissy at the time, but I just was.

"And you're a stupid child, Bull Sheehan," she came right back at me.

"MacUbartutu said something about travelling close to the tail of the snake and the head of the dragon," Tricks said, trying to work out another riddle. Are there stars in the sky called the dragon and the snake?"

"They have noth . . ." Cissy started to dismiss him.

"I wasn't asking you, I was asking Khiddir," Tricks shot her down.

"Eeeeeh . . . enough. It is ma . . . my choice and I choose Scorpio. Weh . . . weh . . . we will follow Scorpio." Jambo stood between myself and Cissy.

"'Make my day, punks!'" Tricks growled as he imitated Clint Eastwood. I think he was delighted by the possibility of a fight between myself and Cissy. "Good on ya Jambo. You tell 'em!"

"Your choice is a good one, oh boy of spirit. Do you see up there?" Khiddir had watched in silence as the four of us bickered and only decided to speak when Jambo had made the decision. He pointed to a group of stars near the Scorpio Gate.

"Yeah!" Tricks said.

"That is the tail of the serpent or snake and almost directly above us is the head of the dragon. They are on the side of Scorpio." Khiddir smiled.

"I knew it," Tricks shouted as he gave me a high five. "Riddleman, has struck again to save the world!"

We all spread out to search around in the dark for the rocks with the star signs carved on them. It was very difficult to see anything but then Jambo decided to catch loads of fireflies in the glass bottle that Missus MacUbartutu had given him to hold the coral in. It was something that he and his brothers used to do for fun when he lived in Africa, he told us.

The trapped and angry fireflies lit up the place like a lamp and soon we had no trouble finding the stone with the stars of Scorpio on it.

Once we knew which path to take we decided to wait until the morning before going into the rainforest. Khiddir said this would be better as the Scorpio Star Path at night would take us very close to the lairs of the snake and dragon and it would be safer if they were asleep.

Most of us were lost in our own thoughts and it was only as the sky began to brighten with the morning sunrise that we started to talk a bit again like. It was a way of easing some of the nerves we felt.

"I'm a Libran," Tricks suddenly said as he got up to stretch. "I've got a balanced personality."

"Yeah!" says I. "Chips on both shoulders. What sign are you Jambo?"

"Leo," Jambo said as he pulled out the fish from his pocket to see if it was alive or dead. It was beginning to smell a bit like.

"And you Cissy?" I asked in turn.

"Mind your own business," she answered bluntly as she headed off into the forest for another pee. She had been in and out of there all night, really annoyed that we had managed to work out the riddle without her.

"Split personality," Tricks whispered as we watched her go. "I think she must be Gemini, the Twins."

I thought of the Noggin twins and wondered if they had survived their encounter with Suzy 'Tulips' O'Farrell. It seemed such a long time ago now.

"What about you, my friend?" Khiddir was looking at me.

"Taurean of course, the Bull," I answered.

"Full of it, more like." Tricks laughed as we waited for Cissy to return before heading up the Scorpio Path.

16

The Colour Green

✳〰ɱ ɱ□●□◆□ ♦□ɱɱ■

Part 3. The Plant of the Heartbeat

The journey up the Scorpio Path of Stealth was a bit like going into a maze and I won't bore you with all the details, except to say that it was hot and steamy like, and Jambo's fish got smellier and smellier. The rainforest was very dark and all the time I felt that something or someone was watching us.

Eventually, we reached the edge of the forest and saw that the path crept up and around the side of a mountain. We trudged happily along until the path began to get narrower and narrower and we were walking almost on the side of a cliff and looking down and down to the ground far below. It was very windy and every now and then one of us would trip on a loose rock and nearly be blown over the edge. We were nearly all as green as Khiddir with the sick feeling we got when we looked down.

"Look ahead of us. Wow! Wicked," Tricks shouted.

We all looked and saw what made him excited. The path had turned around the edge of one mountain and was now heading into a tunnel that disappeared beneath another mountain, which was almost identical to the one we had just climbed. Carved into the rock at either side of the tunnel entrance were two huge scorpions with their tails forming the roof of the tunnel entrance.

THE SCORPION GATES

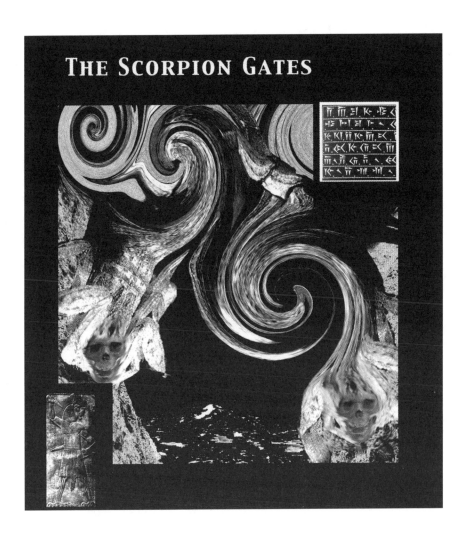

"Wh . . . wh . . . where is this?" Jambo asked.

"These are Mashupitu's twin mountains which guard the rising and setting sun and whose tops support the heavens. The tunnel brings you to the dead world and is guarded by the scorpion-men. Those are the Scorpion Gates!" Khiddir spoke in a very hushed voice. "We must move quickly but once through the far end of the tunnel we are safe. There are twelve doors we have to go through."

Quickly! We ran like mad, ducking under the tails of the

scorpions and entering the tunnel. There was no light coming from the far end and we slowed down to catch our breath when we reached the first set of doors and started to push them open. Something about the stone scorpion-men was bothering me and I kept hearing warning bells in my head like.

"Phew. I didn't like the look of those boyos. Thank goodness they were stone . . ." I stopped speaking as I suddenly remembered where I'd heard the warning. Shimmer had warned us not to turn our backs. ". . . *keep facing the scorpion-men!*" I shouted at the others.

It was too late!

There was a huge screeching noise from the entrance to the tunnel. First the tails and then the bodies of the scorpions came alive and they unwound from the rock and dropped down to the ground of the tunnel path. Their moving legs sounded like a herd of horses as they started slithering after us.

"Ru . . . ru . . . *run!*" Jambo shouted, as he flew past Cissy and me, his big bottom pounding up and down.

"I am running," I shouted back.

No matter how fast we ran the scorpions got closer and closer. Every door we crashed through and closed behind us gained a bit of time but soon the scorpion-men would follow. I could hear their jaws snapping together like scissors when suddenly above us and in front of us their tails appeared. The twelveth and last door was open and beyond it the exit from the tunnel was very close. I could see bright light again. Tricks, Khiddir and Jambo were already through as I tried closing the last door behind me. The tails of the scorpion-men were pushing through and trying to sting us.

I looked ahead towards the exit. Cissy and I were nearly there as well, I thought. The two of us ran even faster and pulled away from the scorpion-men who were just scrambling through the doors. In their annoyance to get after us they knocked one of the doors off its top hinge and the tail of one of

128

the scorpion-men got jammed between the half-toppled door and the wall. He let out a fierce spitting sound as he tried to untangle himself. Cissy was a little bit behind me. We had a chance, I thought like.

Just then, disaster happened like. We were nearly at the exit and nearly free when I stumbled and fell.

Flaming Norah, I thought, I'm a gonner. The stinging tails were getting closer and closer. They were hovering over me about to strike. Sticky saliva was dripping from their mouths. They were sharpening their scissor jaws to chop me up.

Suddenly there was a massive crashing noise. Rocks were falling. Everything was a blur in the dust and mayhem. I could feel arms pulling at me.

I was out the exit and into the light.

"What happened?" I asked. Tricks, was standing over me.

"The roof of the tunnel fell in. Trapped the scorpion-men." He was smiling.

"What about Cissy?" I asked, "Did she get out?"

"Did she what? She's still running and half way down the mountain by now towards the lakes. Probably needs another pee after all that excitement." Tricks laughed.

"Thanks dude," I said gratefully as I sat up and looked out over the valley below us. Everywhere you looked there was another lake, glinting in the sunlight like diamonds.

"We'll be forever finding the right one," I said.

"We best get on with it so?" Tricks agreed.

One by one, Jambo held the fish by its tail into each lake that we met and when it didn't revive marked the lake with a stone cross. We all spread out to make a path to each lake for him to follow after. The land was full of thorn bushes and the skeletons of dead animals around the edge of the water.

I was walking towards another lake when the advice of MacUbartutu, to use the orb-disc, came back to me. I held it up and opened it. The black ball was still in the centre but it suddenly rose and began to move forward. I followed it and we skirted around one more lake before it moved to the centre of another. I noticed that there were no skeletons around this one. At that moment the black ball rose and from it like a large firework display two rainbows burst forth and showered down towards the water. I knew then as I looked at all the wonderful colours spreading out to fill the sky what we were missing from our world. No matter what the dangers, we had to get it back, like.

"This is it," I said quietly to myself. "I've found it. *I've found the 'Water of Life'," I roared.

Suddenly there was a louder roar from another lake behind me. It was Jambo's voice that screamed out and then just as suddenly cut off. 'What's up?' I wondered as I ran in the direction of the sound.

"Where are yous?" I cried out.

"Over here!" a voice replied. When I reached the lake Cissy was already there and Khiddir and Tricks soon arrived.

"What happened? Where's Jambo," I shouted.

Cissy pointed to the lake. She looked horrified. Jambo was lying face down floating on the water, not moving.

"It's a lake of death. He must have fallen in," Khiddir said.

"*I wish that he was safe."* The words were out of my mouth before I knew it and instantly Jambo landed back on the ground beside me. It was the second time he had been saved.

"What happened, Jambo?" Tricks asked.

"I do . . . do . . . don't know. I was walking along and I tripped." He was fierce shook-up like.

"Where's the fish?" I asked.

"In my pocket. Wh . . . wh . . . why?"

"I think I've found the 'Water of Life'," I said, as cool as ice like.

"Where?" Cissy asked, disbelieving me.

They followed after me until we got to the lake I'd found

earlier. It really didn't look any different from all the others except for the lack of skeletons. The rainbows had gone.

"Throw in the fish, Jambo," I said.

Jambo pulled out the fish, which if he wasn't dead before, was now pretty much, after dunk testing in ten or eleven of the death lakes, well and truly cooked. The fish's scales and fins were beginning to peel off and the smell from it was brutal like. Jambo, it must be said, was delighted to be finally rid of it and threw it as far out into the water as he could. For a few moments nothing happened but then we could see it jumping up out of the lake like a dolphin and whizzing round and round like the 'born again' fish it was.

"The Water of Life," Khiddir spoke with some satisfaction, "Come, my friend, Jambo, it is time to dive for the coral. Remember don't drink the water or eat the coral. Living for ever is not all it's supposed to be. Believe me, I know."

While the two of them stripped down to their nicks, Cissy wandered off into the bushes muttering to herself. They were a weird sight together, one green and the other black holding hands as they dived into the water. The ripples made by their splash were more like bands of different colours as they spread across the surface of the water. They seemed to be gone for ages like. Tricks and I stared out over the lake and got a bid worried when the ripples disappeared and there was still no sign of them coming back.

Suddenly there was an explosion of bubbles nearby and up pops Jambo, with a big smile on his face. He was holding what looked like a green thorn bush in his hand and when the sunlight hit it the bush glowed with the brightest green you've ever seen and the reflection off the waters of the lake made everything else, including us, go green as well. He was still smiling as Khiddir surfaced behind him. Khiddir wasn't smiling though.

"*Swim fast.* There is a snake, a very poisionous snake coming after us," Khiddir shouted.

On the surface of the water we could see a red-and-black-striped snake swimming towards them, twisting across the surface. Its jaws were open and it had two sharp fangs. Jambo was closest to the shore and got out quickly. The snake had one look but then ignored Khiddir and raced towards the spot where Jambo was standing. Cissy reappeared from the bushes nearby.

"Throw the coral to me, Jambo. The snake will follow it and I know how to deal with them," she shouted.

"Forget the coral, Cissy. Just come and get the snake," Jambo whispered keeping one eye on the snake and walking backwards away from it.

"No. Give me the coral first," she insisted.

Jambo looked like he was about to but then changed his mind. By now he was dancing backwards, a bit like Chief Crazy Watercourse, away from the snake. There was a large rock behind him.

"Watch out, Jambo!" I shouted.

Too late! Jambo tripped over the rock and fell on his back. He held on tightly to the coral. The snake looked like it was smiling as it reached and then began slithering up one of Jambo's legs. Reaching his tummy, the snake suddenly arched its neck and its tongue darted out making a hissing sound.

"It's going to strike," Tricks shouted.

"Flaming Norah!" I shouted, helpless to do anything. "Cissy and you still have . . ." I started to say when a sudden whooshing screech went flying past my ear.

"It . . . it's Shimmer's screech-owl," Tricks said for all of us.

It swooped low over the ground and flying across Jambo's shaking tummy snatched up the snake with its talons and landed nearby, where it began to tear the snake asunder, starting with the tail. Cissy moved forward to try and stop it doing this but the owl screeched at her and flew up in flurry of feathers and snakeskin to sit on a nearby tree. When it had finished doing the snake in like, we watched with tummy-churning faces while it began to eat the pieces stopping every now and then to let out an even louder screech.

Jambo got up slowly and while he recovered from yet another near-death experience Tricks and I broke up the coral into small pieces and put them into the glass bottle of Missus MacUbartutu.

"I'll look after it, if you like," Cissy the snake lover offered with a sullen look back at the screech owl.

"No thank you," Jambo said defiantly. "It's my colour and I think its time to call up the whirlwind." Jambo, I noticed, had said all this without a single stutter as he typed in ◆⌇◆□◆□□☺&.

As I handed MacUbartutu's disc-orb to Khiddir the whirlwind formed. Even he was impressed like and as it wrapped around us the Shimmer's owl flew into it as well to land on my shoulder. The last we saw of Khiddir was him waving up at us from the ground below.

Cissy, Tricks, Jambo and I were delighted to be back at the Faery School again, as was Shimmer when she saw that we had her screech-owl with us. She gave us all a kiss, but I think mine lasted longer than the others like. The screech-owl winked at me as she did this and went 'Whoahooo . . . whoahoooo'.

Jambo typed in 'Raincolour' and once the time-tunnel opened, we were soon back at home.

This time we had been gone for nearly five cowers and Puffer was delighted to see us return. Knackered, we headed home to eat, but even that was difficult in that the DSS girls wanted to lock us up for breaking the curfew.

17

THE COLOUR BLUE

✳〰〖 〗□●□◆□ 〖●◆〖

The JinkJinn and disappearing Tricks

Tricks, Cissy and I were standing at the map wall and were ready to go. Puffer and Mister Penhaligan were also there and had spent a lot of time with us discussing the last trip. Atlas, Jambo, and Kegs had come along to wave us off and perhaps, with the exception of Jambo, were disappointed that they couldn't go as well.

Sheevra said she couldn't come to the school because she was having her hair done up for a big parade that Devine's Shadowtime Soldiers were putting on for the visit of IL DOCE and Queen-to-be, Katie Allteeth to the town. If I'd hoped that all our adventures would change her a bit then I would be waiting a long time.

Atlas had managed to sneak Kegs out of the Happy Gulag pretending that he was needed to help Mister Murphy roll out beer barrels for target practice for the Chameleon tanks. When he got home there was some very interesting news. Apparently, Missus Murphy told him with a big grin on her face, Norah O'Toole and Sergeant Ulysses Finnegan had struck up a great friendship in the lock-up and were last seeing hitching a ride, from the television repair van, out of town. We learnt later that Mister Murphy was so devastated that he had smashed up his own television, completely like.

134

Things were also getting much worse in the rest of the country and the world. The Department of Indian Affairs, now under IL DOCE's direct command, threatened to blast a town in the west of the country with sidewinder missiles, because a small child had written to them asking what was the difference between a 'Red' Indian and a Native American Indian. It was amazing to realise how a simple colour word could cause so much anger but then most people were going psycho from the loss of colour and nearly all the adults suffered in some way from SHAGDED disorder.

"Com'on you lot. Get going would ya!" Kegs said.

"Yes, it is important that you leave quickly. We all wish you the very best of good fortune and hope that you return safely," Jambo said without a single stutter. We all looked at him in amazement.

"Where's your stutter gone?" Cissy asked in a way that I thought she wanted to remind him of it.

"Since coming back with the Green, Samuel Kitangiri has become a man. I no longer fear what's out there. The stutter has gone," Jambo said with a big smile.

"Any chance of lending me your deep voice so, Jambo?" Tricks laughed. "I might have better luck with the big girls in the DSS."

"No, my friend, I'll try and use it myself for a while." Jambo went around the room giving 'high fives' to everyone, well everyone except Cissy that is, who was busy as usual checking the message box on her phone.

"See you later, Puffer," Tricks said as he typed in '**Raincolour**' on his phone and then turned to place his hand on Timbuktu.

"Good bye, Mister Kirby. Good luck," Puffer replied. "Remember, the woman you are looking for is called Shahrazade."

Puffer seemed sad as he said this, with wrinkles quivering all over the place, and I wondered why at the time. I felt a weird icy chill go down my back as I placed my hand over Tricks and Cissy Hourihan's.

We were soon standing in the schoolroom of the Faery World. Shimmer was there to meet us, as was her owl, which gave me a big wink.

"Hello, my friends. The fifth journey starts." Shimmer smiled. "Whom do you seek?"

"Shahrazade," Tricks said.

"She is a thousand nights and one from here. Call up the whirlwind and whisper *'Babul'*. She will be waiting for you in the Light Garden." Suddenly Shimmer was gone and the only noise we could hear was the *kaouan* screech of her owl.

Tricks took out his phone and began to tap in the FDTL letters '✎☙♌♋◆●'.

Before we go any further I'd better tell you a bit more about James 'Tricks' Kirby. He was a small fellow with red hair, freckles, and always wore shoes that were too big for him, thinking that he'd grow into them. His dad, being a farmer, spoke like a farmer and used to call Tricks the runt of the litter. He had four bigger brothers and two even larger sisters but they were much older than him. They also called him 'runt' and when James started in the school he was teased and bullied by bigger boys.

He never cried but learnt to do tricks and pull funny faces that made everybody laugh. Soon everyone wanted him in their gang and stopped bullying him. Once, and I think I might have told you this already, Tricks stayed in the graveyard for a whole night. He said he wanted to pull faces at the devil and spit in the eye of the weasel that the devil rode through the graveyard.

He never, ever said what happened that night, but he was fierce brave to do it like. When we were too shy, he was the one who had the big girls in the secondary school drooling all over us. He said they did it because he was colourful not colour seeing.

136

Of all the lads I liked Tricks the best. We had been friends forever like, and he was rearing to go.

The whirlwind appeared and we joined hands again. It twisted round and round us until Tricks shouted '*Babul*' at he top of his voice. He was never one to whisper. The next thing we knew we were standing on the top of a very high mountain looking down at a really blue river, far, far, below us. It was cold, with snow everywhere and very, very bright.

"I shouldn't have borrowed Sheevra's shades." Tricks grinned, as he pulled a pair of expensive sunglasses from his pocket. "But, I knew they'd come in handy."

"She'll kill you," Cissy said.

"Where are we?" I wondered.

"You are looking into Nuristan, the land of light." A voice from behind spoke. We all turned to see a girl, wearing what looked like a big tent, smiling at us. You could only see her eyes and a little of her tummy. She had big brown eyes and a small inny belly button.

"Are you Shahrazade?" Cissy asked.

"Yes. What do you want here?" she asked.

"We're looking for the colour Blue?" I said.

"Who is the seeker?" She lifted the tent so we could see all her face. She was very young and very beautiful.

"I am." Tricks winked at her. Mister 'colourful' Kirby was up to his tricks again.

"Why do you want blue?" She asked.

We told her about the loss of colour in our world and how we were trying to get it back.

"Are you able to help us?" I asked.

"Perhaps!" She turned to look at Tricks. "Will you tell me something?"

"Anything," Tricks mumbled. His tongue was hanging out of his mouth, like a thirsty dog, and his eyes were staring. Big girls had that effect on him. It was sad like, and I had to give him a large dig, to get him to cop himself on.

"Why?" Shahrazade asked again.

"Because I hate red." Tricks spat this out. It seemed a strange reason to like a colour to me.

"I don't understand," Shahrazade said. Neither did I.

"When I was small my mother dressed me in a stupid red jumper and red socks for my first day at school. She'd got it all wrong. Everyone else was wearing blue. That day was the first time I knew that she was blue – red colour blind and confused the two. It wasn't her fault really but the bigger boys started picking on me straightaway because of that red jumper. I so wanted to be blue like the other kids. I also like the night-time. I understand things better when I think of blue." Tricks stopped for breath. We were very high in the mountains and the air was very thin. "I like you," he wheezed.

"I like you too, Mister Tricky and will therefore tell you where to find the Blue colour you seek." Shahrazade lent forward and kissed him on the forehead. Tricks went red, the colour he hated.

"Where?" Cissy spoke sharply but Shahrazade ignored her as she took Tricks' hand.

"Do you see the blue river down there. You must follow it until you come to the cliffs of white marble. Buried in these white marble walls are secret pockets of a special stone called Lapis Lazuli. Lazuli when crushed and washed is the ultramarine blue, the blue from beyond the sea. It is the most precious blue and the blue of light." Her voice was dreamy. "That is the Blue you seek."

"It's a long way down. It would be nice if just once we could use a whirlwind for a second time," I said.

"Not possible," Cissy said.

"In any event, and remember this when you want to leave, whirlwinds don't work in these valleys. You will have to ride the

Monk's trail on the back of my snow leopard." Shahrazade pointed to a white leopard, that was walking up the hill towards us. "He will carry you as far as the Bridge of Sorrows. From there you will have to walk."

The leopard waited for us until we all climbed on its back. Tricks had to be pulled away from Shahrazade. He was puckering his lips for another kiss.

"Please," he whined. "We mightn't see each other ever again."

Shahrazade suddenly looked sad, a bit like Puffer was when we were back in the schoolroom. "Be very careful my friends. Watch your backs." She only looked at Tricks and me and I'd spent enough time watching me back already. I don't think Cissy and her saw eye to eye. How unusual like, I thought.

The journey down the Monk's trail was very twisty and very slow. I could see why it was called that because the snow all around us had heaped up into frozen mounds that looked like a load of snowmen dressed like praying monks. We eventually got to the river and reached the Bridge of Sorrows. The leopard left us there.

It wasn't really a bridge but a large tree that had fallen over a narrow gap in the mountains. Way below us the river thundered through the gap and the noise was frightening. We crossed it very slowly, as it was very slippery from the spray coming up from the river. I could see why it was called the Bridge of Sorrows. One wrong move and you were history, man.

A little beyond the bridge we turned a corner to be faced by a whole cliff made of white stone. There were people working there, sticking planks of wood into cracks in the cliff and then setting the wood on fire.

As we got close a large part of the cliff started to split away. It fell in huge chunks all around us, and one chunk sent Tricks toppling like a skittle in a bowling alley. Shaking his head as he got up, Tricks looked around to see what had hit him. He saw that it was a ball of blue stone, which when he picked it up and held it to the light also had flecks of gold that glittered. As Atlas might have said, the colour had found him.

"*Lazuli*, Lazuli." The men who had been working on the cliff were shouting as they ran towards us. They looked very angry.

"*Flaming Norah!*" I said as they surrounded us, shaking their fists at us.

"What do they want?" Tricks asked.

"It's their stone. I'd say they want a swop for it," Cissy said.

"I've got nothing to swop." Tricks sounded worried. The fists were getting closer.

"Yes, you have. Your mobile phone! Give them that," Cissy ordered.

"But we'll need it to get out of here," I said.

"No we don't. Once we have the Blue, Bull and I can call up the whirlwind," she said bossily.

"Are you sure?" Tricks asked.

"Certain," Cissy replied. "Now hurry."

So Tricks swapped his titanium phone for the blue Lazuli stone, which one of the miners then crushed into a very fine powder and started pouring like salt into an ugly-looking bag made of a goatskin. I poked at the bag with my nose turned up.

"*Buzkashi, buzkashi,*" the old miner in a flat cap kept saying as he smiled at me. I think it was a smile.

"What does he mean by *buzkashi*?" Tricks asked.

"It's a game they play here," Cissy said, "where they drag a dead goat from one end of a field to another on horseback."

"*Flaming Norah!*" I said, looking at the bag. "That would get up the goat of any poor goat."

The miners were very proud of the goatskin bag but were just as happy to take the phone as a swop when I picked it up and pretended to play a game of football with it.

"*Phonekashi, phonekashi,*" I shouted. Since it was made of

140

titatanium and indestructible maybe they could play with that instead, I thought. I was sort of day-dreaming that the goats of the world would appreciate my efforts until Cissy spoke.

"Stop jumping around like a silly goat, Bull Sheehan. We need to get going," she said bossily.

Tricks hesitated however. He was really annoyed about having to give up his phone and it wasn't because of the whirlwind. He had managed to put in all the telephone numbers of the big DSS girls in its memory.

Sad, really!

It was getting quite dark as we got near the bridge and it was also weirdly quiet like. No sound of water, or birds or wind. We walked nervously looking around us, thinking something was about to happen.

Suddenly a voice spoke!

We nearly jumped out of our own skins. There was a little old man sitting on the end of the bridge. He had very, very dark eyes and hairy skin and arms that were longer than his body. He reminded me of the orangutangs I once saw in the zoo. He was about half my size and all his bones were sticking out.

"Hello, my young friends. Do an old man a favour and help me across the bridge. My legs are too shaky to cross by myself." His voice was strong for someone who looked so sick.

"How?" I asked.

"Take me on your shoulders," he said. We all looked at each other.

"I'll take him," Tricks volunteered.

"No, I'll do it. You have the crushed blue stone to carry," I said, regretting that I did so, straight away like. "Cissy you go first, Tricks will follow and I'll come last with your man here. Ok!" I bent down to let the old fellow climb on. He hopped on very fast for someone who looked so frail. "What's your name old man?"

141

JINKJINN

"JinkJinn," he replied.

Maybe old people do that a lot, I thought. Whenever I asked my granny what she liked doing the most she would say 'dink gin' as well.

When it was my turn to cross the Bridge of Sorrows the tree bark seemed to get more and more slippery and it was difficult to keep my footing. The old man, JinkJinn, was rocking from side to side on my shoulders and nearly causing me to lose my balance and fall into the rushing water of the river below. The crashing noise, coming up from the river, got louder and louder and my heart beat faster and faster. I was severely worried like, but JinkJinn was laughing like a sick hyena. The crossing took me ages and when I eventually crawled to the far side, with him riding on my back like a demented jockey, there was no sign of Tricks or Cissy.

"You can get down now," I said to the old fellow. My ribs were sore from where he had dug his legs in. "We're across."

"No! I'm staying on your back," JinkJinn said in a rasping voice. His legs tightened around my neck.

"No you're not. I'm in a hurry and must join my friends. I've done what you asked." I was getting angry.

"You have done much more than was asked of you, my young friend. Look at all the trouble you caused in the City of Skeleton's and stealing our *tibar*," he rasped.

"Your *tibar*. What do you mean?" I croaked.

"I am JinkJinn, King of the Jinn. It was from our island and it was our *tibar* that you stole and now you will pay." He was hissing mad by this stage.

"*Gerroff* my back, you ugly ape," I shouted while trying to pull his legs from around my neck.

"I'm staying right here," he said as his legs tightened around my neck some more. I could suddenly see his feet. They were shaped like a goat's hoof. "But I need to urinate."

"Well get off then!" I screamed.

"No need. I'll do it here."

I could feel hot liquid running down my back and wetting my pants. It smelt really awful, like sour yoghurt.

"Yuk! That's gross," I said.

"Ahhhhh! That's better," he groaned.

"Bull."

I could hear my name being shouted from near where the river flowed past the bottom of the path. It sounded like Tricks' voice. I began to run, which was very difficult with JinkJinn wanting to go in a different direction. He suddenly had developed a tail, which was wrapping itself around my legs. I tripped and we tumbled down the path to the riverbank. He never let his grip on my back relax. I looked around for Tricks.

"Tricks. Where are you? *Help me!*" I cried. The echoes bounced back from the gorge walls. JinkJinn was squeezing my neck even harder.

"Over here." I heard a faint shout.

"Where?" I croaked, like a frog.

"In the river, Bull. Over here!" Tricks' voice was weak. I looked at the river for a long time until I spotted him clinging onto a small rock on the far side. A little further ahead the river was crashing into rapids made of needle-sharp rocks.

"What happened?" I croaked again.

"I don't know. I was waiting for you when I felt a gush of wind, lost my balance and fell in," he shouted back.

"Where's Cissy?" I wondered.

"Don't know?" he said. "Must have gone on ahead, I think. The snow leopard was waiting and Cissy was across the bridge very fast." There was a pause. "Bull!" He sounded worried.

"Yes, Tricks," I shouted while trying to shake JinkJinn off my back.

"I won't be able to hold on much longer."

"Right," I said, "I wish . . ." but then remembered I'd used it to save Jambo. In any event, my words were cut off by

JinkJinn squeezing as hard as he could on my neck. He started ranting and raving.

"Sink, sink you tricky wink. Blink, blink and drown in drink," he heckled.

"Why are you laughing Bull? It's not funny," Tricks shouted.

"It's not me, honestly like. The old geezer we met at the bridge is still on my back and won't let go. I think he wants to squeeze the life out of me. He even peed down my back and I'm choking," I croaked again, as the leg crush got tighter and tighter.

Suddenly he was gone.

JinkJinn tumbled off my back and into the water. There was a hissing sound and loads of steam where he fell in. The water around him turned black. The current quickly pulled him away and into the rapids where the sharp rocks cut him up into thousands of parts. The last part to go was his voice, which screamed out curses and dirty words until it too was washed away.

"What happened?" I wondered as I felt my sore neck.

"I used my wish to get him off your back," Tricks called over.

"Thanks, dude. Now I'll come in and get you," I said.

"No! Don't Bull," Tricks shouted out as loud as he could.

"Why not?" I was wading into the river to see if I could get closer to him. The current was very strong.

"The river is too strong. We need to save the blue Lazuli stone. The bag fell off when I toppled into the river and it's wedged between two small rocks behind me but the force of the water is squeezing it through the gap. I can just about reach the bag before it goes off into the rapids, if I let go of the rock. You must save the Blue, Bull."

"Don't do it, Tricks," I shouted.

"No choice, Bull. I'm going to let go of the rock, grab the bag and throw it to you. You must catch that!" His voice was calm. "Don't worry about me."

"No I won't, James Kirby. I'll save you before the stupid colour. Don't be mad." I was starting to cry.

"Listen to me, Bull! We all came here to help our world and not each other. You must save the bag. We must get the colours back. *Are you ready!*"

Where was Cissy? I wondered. We could use her wish to save Tricks. I tapped out a message on my phone. There was no response.

"Tricks, hold on. I'll come around again by the bridge," I cried out. I knew I couldn't do anything else. Where the hell was Cissy?

"Bull. No. Get the bag now or it will be too late. *Now Bull!* Do this for me," Tricks pleaded.

At that very moment Tricks let the rock go and, despite being pulled by the current, he stretched out his hand to grab the goatskin bag and throw it into the air. It landed on the bank beside me.

"*I have it, Tricks.* I have it. Grab another rock. Hold on will ya, hold on until Cissy comes back," I screamed.

"Goodbye, Bull. Its so friggin' cold I can't hold on any longer. Tell my mum and dad, and the girls in the secondary school, I love them. I'll see ya. You were the best pal anyone could have." His voice got fainter and fainter.

"Tricks! *Tricks are you there?*" I screamed again.

There was no answer this time, just the sound of the river water crashing into the rapids and my sobbing tears splattering onto the rocks.

I sat there for ages, crying like, until the snow leopard came alongside and started licking the tears away with his tongue. I climbed onto his back, holding the bag of powdered blue stone as tightly as I could.

I didn't really care if I fell off or not.

18

THE COLOUR INDIGO

❄〰♏︎ ♏︎□●□◆□ ♛■♋♒♓♌□

Part 1. The big F, Freybensky shows himself

Cissy was waiting for me at the top of the mountain pass. Shahrazade was standing beside her but they weren't speaking. As the leopard had run all the way up the hill he was panting like mad when we stopped.

I was still crying when they came over to see what was wrong.

"What happened?" Cissy asked.

"Where is your friend?" Shahrazade asked.

I told them what had happened to Tricks but suddenly, very angry, I turned on Cissy.

"*Where were you?* Why didn't you wait for us? I tried texting you but you didn't answer." The questions came flying out.

"The leopard was waiting when I crossed and because we were going uphill he only wanted to take one of us at a time. I got on straightaway and came here to wait," Cissy answered. "Anyway, like whirlwinds, the text signal doesn't work in that valley. I wouldn't be able to get a message."

"Is that true?" I looked at Shahrazade, who nodded sadly. She touched my shoulder.

"I must go now! I wish you luck, Bull Sheehan." As the words finished the light around her became very bright and she

147

and the snow leopard seemed to merge with the snow. They disappeared before our very eyes leaving Cissy and me looking at each other.

"You can use your wish now to bring Tricks back," I said.

"Don't you remember, Bull, I used up my wish in the tunnel, when we were being chased by the scorpion-men, to cause the roof to fall in." she said sweetly.

"What?" I asked, a little confused. "Is that what happened?"

"Yes, but you were probably a bit too dazed to remember. There was a lot of noise," she said.

"I don't remember. So much has happened I suppose," I sighed. "I'm sorry if I didn't thank you. I just didn't realise you had done it like."

"It's ok. We'd best get going."

"Yeah. You'd better call up the whirlwind to take us back to the school. I don't know what we're going to say to Tricks' family or Puffer when we get back."

"We're not going back to the school, Bull." Cissy stood up. "I'm going to text Puffer to see where we're to go to next."

"Why?" I said.

"Remember that with Tricks gone we can only use the timehole once, to bring two colours back together. We'll go and get Indigo and bring Blue back at the same time." She started texting Puffer.

'⚓︎☉❖︎♏︎ ⬧︎●︎❖︎♏︎ ♌︎♦︎♦ ❅︎□︎♓︎♍︎⬧︎♐ ○︎♓︎⬧︎⬧︎♓︎■︎⅄︎☝ ♦□︎♓︎■︎⅄︎ ✖︎□︎□︎ ✋︎■︎♎︎♓︎⅄︎□︎☝ ♦︎♓︎❖︎♏︎ □︎☉︎⬧︎⬧︎♦︎□︎□︎⚏ ✖︎□︎□︎ ❖︎〰︎♓︎□︎●︎❖︎♓︎■︎⚏ – Have Blue but Tricks missing. Going for Indigo. Give password for whirlwind –' She tapped out.

Puffer answered straight away. I looked over Cissy's shoulder. The message read '⍟❖︎⅄︎☉︎□︎⚏. (Asgard). ♇︎〰︎☉︎♦ 〰︎☉︎□︎□︎♏︎■︎♏︎⚏? (What happened?)'

"You call up the whirlwind Cissy while I tell him," I said as I started to tap out the message on my phone. Suddenly, she pulled it from my hand and turned it off. "What gives like?" I asked crossly.

"You'll need to save your battery, Bull. We won't be able to recharge as we're not going home. We'll tell him all about it later. Let's go," she grunted as she handed it back to me.

I knew she was right and that it was a good idea to go on for her colour. The whirlwind was forming and throwing the snow in every direction as it came closer. As we waited for it to suck us in, Cissy had a real weird smile on her face.

Cissy Hourihan was taller than the rest of us. As my Mum would say, she was very mature for her age. In fact she was taller and more mature than many of the girls in the secondary school. Tricks said she was probably stealing some of the drugs that her father, the vet, used for animals. 'Angel dust' was mentioned but Cissy looked anything but an angel.

She had jet-black hair that nearly reached her waist and always wore a silver chain with a two-headed man on it around her neck.

She spent a lot of time in her room studying old magic books and the stories of long ago. Her pet snakes, called Loki and Odin, needed loads of mice to eat and every evening you would see Cissy coming from the fields with a bag full of mice that she had caught in her traps. Some were still alive and squealed like mad. She ignored them.

Cissy was not a person you wanted to meet on a dark night, particularly if you were a mouse.

"Hold it, Cissy!" I suddenly shouted. "We don't know who we're to meet. Shimmer didn't tell us. Let me text Puffer again."

"No need to. I already know!" Cissy said matter of factly.

The whirlwind was by now all around us. It sucked at my clothes and the goatskin bag of the blue powder that I had slung over my shoulder. Cissy whispered the password '**Asgard**' and in an instant we were on the side of another mountain, somewhere else.

There was a huge house built of logs just ahead of where we stood and a tall man with golden-yellow hair tied in plaits was pounding his way towards us. He looked like Puffer, only much taller but with the same bad dress sense. The weirdest thing about him like, was that he seemed to have two faces. Whereas Puffer's wrinkles would dart all over his face, this dude's just went from one side to the other. It looked like he had two completely different faces.

"*Flaming Norah,*" I said. "Where are we?"

"Norway, and that man is Freybensky." Cissy started to walk towards the giant.

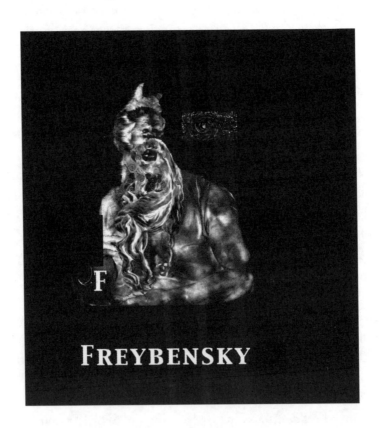

FREYBENSKY

"How do you know his name?" I asked.

"Because he is waiting for me?" She looked back. "We met in a chat room."

"What kind of chat room did you meet him in?" I sneered. "The WGF (World Gurning Federation) one, was it?" Some of the girls in the school used to love the gurning (A competition for pulling horrible faces like, where some people could pull their lips over their noses.) programmes on the television. Suzy 'Tulips' O'Farrell said she had learnt all her best moves from watching the WGF.

This giant of a man was not a pretty sight however and I bet he never posted his picture up on the web page.

"Shut up, Bull Sheehan. What right have you to say something like that?" Cissy said.

"Meeting someone from a chat room is dangerous Cissy. Everyone knows that. You might meet a weirdo. . . like him. Anyway, how would you know how to contact someone in the Faery World?" I whispered, as the man got closer.

"When the rains came I knew something was going on. Then the colour went and I, from reading my Wicca books realised what was happening. In a strange way all my life I'd been waiting for this to happen. I contacted the 'Bifrost . netgrid' web site and in the chat room Freybensky introduced himself. It's like he's the only person I know who really understands me. That's why I chose Indigo. It's his favourite colour. He says it represents the very highest qualities of loyalty and trust."

Unlikely, I thought, as he stood in front of us. My eyes were just level with his knees and I could see that he had a huge scar running down the side of one leg. Suddenly he began jumping up and down, fierce excited like. His voice boomed and the ground moved.

"My *greta*, Cissy, you have come at last! How is it in your world?" He held out a hand the size of a large plate for Cissy to take.

"Dark and misty," she said.

"A pity," he said. "The People of the Shadow Lands are very dangerous. They will stop at nothing to destroy your world."

"What's going on?" I shouted. "What does he mean by *'my greta, Cissy'*, anyway?"

She looked back at me for a moment, as if I was a blot on the landscape.

"I'm to be his wife, Bull, we're engaged to be married." Cissy smiled up at the giant Freybensky as she squeezed a cucumber-sized finger.

"Yeah sure, Cissy! Give us a break, will ya? Cop yourself on like! You're too young to be married," I said, sure of myself.

"Not here, Bull. Not here in Asgard! That's why I came. Freybensky is the only person I could marry. He really knows me!" Cissy spat out.

"Who is this small turd, you have brought with you, my greta Cissy." Freybensky glared down at me.

"That is Bull Sheehan. He tells stories," Cissy replied.

"Well my little Skald. Why did you come here?" he asked.

"We came looking for a colour. Our world is in Shadow and we have to save it," I said nervously.

"Hei! Hei! You came to the right place so, for all the good it will do." He laughed in a rotten, sinister way and turned away.

"Why?" I shouted while pulling at a hair on his leg to get him to stop. It wasn't a good move and I soon found myself lifted up and held under his arm. The smell of sweat from his armpit was gross.

"Do you see over there, Skald?" Freybensky pointed me, not his finger, so that I could see. There was a beautiful rainbow bridge crossing a huge waterfall that came out of a gap in the mountains.

"Yes," I squeaked.

"That is the *Bifrost*, the rainbow bridge between Asgard and those in the Shadowlands. I am the guardian of that bridge. Do not think you can steal the colour you want from me." He roared out laughing. "We must hurry, the wedding feast is set for tomorrow and there is much to be done."

With Freybensky's huge legs we soon reached the massive hall of the Asgard and I was thrown in with the suckling pigs, which were waiting to be cooked, and who didn't like the smell of the goatskin bag I had with me. An evil-looking dwarf kept watch on me, his eyes could move in different directions at once.

Cissy had disappeared with Freybensky and the rest of the day the hall was full of people getting the tables and decorations ready for a huge party. I was getting more and more frightened when suddenly one of the pigs managed to escape from the cook and he and the dwarf had to chase round the room after it. I pulled out my phone.

Cissy was right. My battery was very low. I tapped in '⚐◆ⵊⵊⅢ□⊞ ⚑⚿■⅋Ⅲ□ ⵋ■ ⚡◆⅋⚿□⌁⊞ ⚷□ ◆ⵋ◆ⵌⅢ◆ ●Ⅲⵌ◆⊞ ◆Ⅲ■⚔ ℙⅢ●□◿ -.' Puffer, Danger in Asgard, No wishes left, Send Help!-.'

"Hurry, Puffer," I whispered, as the low battery warning noise sounded. The dwarf heard and was coming back to investigate.

'⊛□⚔◆□ ⅏□○⚿■⅋!' (Lodur coming!)

The message flashed. I shut down the phone and hid it in my trousers. The dwarf stood in front of me and was grinning evilly.

"We've lost one of the pigs so you'll have to do, Skald. Time for the pot." He grabbed me by the collar. "I'll take that!" He pulled the bag of blue powder from my grip. "None of us like the taste of blue goat. Hei! Hei!" he cackled as he pulled me towards where a large fire was burning. The fat cook was waiting.

"You'll need to skewer him first," the cook slobbered. She handed the dwarf what looked like a long metal spear.

"Now where will I push it in first," the dwarf cackled again. "Down the mouth or up the bottom? Down the mouth I think. After all he is a storyteller."

"Yeah. Down the mouth!" The cook giggled.

The dwarf pinned me between his legs and was lifting my head up by putting two fingers in my nostrils. The spear tip was coming closer and closer. I didn't want to be skewered. I must have fainted with the fright.

19

THE COLOUR INDIGO

☼〰ᛗ ᛗ□●□◆□ ♑■♌〈ᚋ□

Part 2. The Wedding at Asgard

When I woke up I was lying in the middle of the hall sitting in a puddle of water. Somebody was standing over me with a empty bucket in his hand.

"Are you all right, Skald?" a gentle voice asked.

"They . . . they were going to skewer and cook me," I stuttered.

"I've had a word with them. They said they were only playing a game with you. Wanted to frighten you a little. They have never seen anyone from the other world before," the voice continued.

I couldn't see his face as his head was in the centre of the evening sun that shone through the open door of the hall. I could just make out the cackling figures of the dwarf and the cook standing near the fire. They were laughing at me and slapping each other on the back as they skewered another pig.

"Who are you?" I asked.

"I am Lodur. Now stand up and come to my room where you can dry off. I want you to tell me your story." He took my hand and I got up and walked with him to a room at the end of the hall. It had a huge fire and soon my clothes were dry.

Lodur had a long white beard and pointed nose and eyes that changed colour every few moments. He wore a long red

GALWAY COUNTY LIBRARIES

cape, which dragged on the ground behind him as he walked about the room listening to my story. I told him everything, how we had come to Asgard for Indigo, and how Cissy was going to marry Freybensky. When I said this he looked very worried.

"Oh! You'll need to warn her to try and get away. Freybensky picks out a young girl every year from somewhere in Faery World but only so that he can send them across the Bifrost Bridge into the Land of Shadows. That is his deal with Skathanna. The girls do not become his own wife but become the wives of the Salmon Kings who do the evil work of Skathanna. He has no choice in this matter, even if he likes your friend Cissy more than all the other girls he's brought here," Lodur said gravely, shaking his head.

"What do you mean?" I asked.

"I think Freybensky really wants to hold onto your friend Cissy, probably because she is from your world. It was him that caused all the trouble in your quest. It was him that tried to poison your friend Jambo and have the slave traders try and smother you in sand. It was him that pushed your friend Tricks into the river and who released the snake at the Water of Life. He has followed your every move." Lodur put his hand on my shoulder.

"All those messages from someone called **F** on Cissy's phone. It *was* him all along, wasn't it? I knew someone was trying to stop us. *I just knew it.*" I shuddered with anger when I thought of what he had done to Tricks.

"Yes." Lodur nodded his head.

"Why?" I was nearly crying.

"He didn't want you to succeed. He was afraid that if you did, then Cissy, the first girl he has managed to get here from your world, would be lost to him."

"So what happens now?" I sobbed.

"Every year before the handover of the selected girl there is a mock battle between warriors of Asgard and those of the

Shadowlands. That is what all the preparations are for. All of our warriors are gathering here tonight for a feast before the fight with the Salmon Kings." Lodur sat down and looked into the fire as he spoke. "At this moment I think Freybensky is probably trying to figure out how to avoid Cissy being handed across the bridge to the Salmon Kings. Like I said, he has no choice and our people will demand that he does so. That is our way."

"Why didn't Puffer warn us? We could have used one of our wishes to get rid of him." I was getting mad like.

"He couldn't, wouldn't." Lodur didn't look at me but just kept staring at the fire.

"Why?" I asked.

"Freybensky is his brother," Lodur said quietly.

Flaming Norah!" I said before putting my hands over my eyes and rocking back and forth. I had now a flaming headache and it was a few minutes before I could speak again.

"Why don't you stop the handover, Lodur?" I asked.

"When both our worlds were very young it was I who gave the first peoples warmth and colour in their lives. But now I am old and Freybensky is more powerful," Lodur said sadly.

"There must be something you can do?" I jumped up. "We must do something!"

"I've had a thought?" Lodur, suddenly said as a spark flew out from the fire.

"What is it?" I asked.

"Tonight, before the feast starts, the warriors will paint on their sacred paint which they use to ward off the evil spirits. This paint is the Indigo colour you are looking for. It is made from the woad plant, a plant from the mustard family, and is very sacred to the people of Asgard," Lodur said quietly.

"Where is this woad?" I asked.

"With your friend Cissy. Freybensky has given it to her to paint her face. When she marries she will have a woadfull glow," he answered.

"What will we do so?" I was trying to figure out a plan of action like.

"Later, when Freybensky and the other warriors are all drunk, you must sneak out, and leave with your friend Cissy. If she's not here then there can be no battle." Lodur was nodding his head.

"Where's Cissy?" I asked.

"In the tower. I'll show you a secret way but we must wait until they are all drunk," Lodur whispered.

It was much later when the feast began. When all of the huge warriors of Asgard came into the hall they were painted with the woad paint and the thick indigo coloured strokes made their faces even uglier and more frightening than before. Soon they began eating and drinking, and singing and drinking, and telling stories and drinking but mainly drinking from huge big tubs into which they dipped their sheep-horn cups. Freybensky was singing louder and drinking more than all of them put together like, but he didn't look a happy giant like. Maybe Lodur was right about him really wanting to hold onto Cissy. If that was the case then there would be a real battle instead of a mock one. The warriors all got very drunk and one by one collapsed onto the floor.

"Now, Bull Sheehan. Go now!" Lodur whispered.

I waited until it was very quiet and tiptoed out of Lodur's room and past the tables of snoring warriors. They sounded very much like Kegs Murphy's adopted dad, only worse. The goatskin of blue lazuli was sitting beside the fire and I had to sneak it out from under the noses of the sleeping cook and dwarf. I resisted, fierce hard, giving them both a kick like.

Outside the hall, Lodur was waiting and led me to a secret passageway that climbed up the side of the tower. Cissy was very surprised when he and I came through the mirror in her room. She was dressed in white and rings of daisies were plaited into her hair. She was also blue in the face from painting on the woad and there was a fierce smell in the room, which got stronger as I moved close to her.

"Cissy, we've got to go? You're in danger!" I pleaded with her.

"No I'm not," she said bossily. "Go away Bull. I'm busy getting ready for my wedding."

"There is no wedding, Cissy. Freybensky doesn't intend to marry you. He is setting you up like."

"You're lying, Bull. What would you know about it?"

"Tell her Lodur. Tell her about the handover. Tell her about what Freybensky did to our friends," I said urgently.

Lodur began to tell her and at first Cissy didn't want to believe him either.

"You're lying as well!" she snapped at him.

It was only when he started to mention the other girls that Freybensky had brought here from chat rooms in Faery World and who had never been seen again that, I thought, she began to see some sense.

"Listen, Cissy, if you don't believe us, text Puffer and ask him. Freybensky's his brother," I pleaded.

"You're joking, Bull. F would have told me." She was a little unsure as she pulled out her phone and started texting Puffer. The answer soon came back.

'✋⧫'⬧ ⧫❒◆♏. ☞♏ ♓⬧ ⧫♒♏ ⧫⬥□-⌠♋♍♏♎ ❍♏❍♌♏❒ □⌠ □◆❒ ⌠♋❍♓●⍓. ✋ ♋❍ ⬧□❒❒⍓.' It read out. Cissy translated. "It's true. He is the two-faced member of our family. I am sorry. Puffer." She looked at it for a long time before turning to me.

"I didn't know. I didn't know, Bull. I'm so sorry about Tricks. It's all my fault." She was crying.

I searched around the room for the jar of woad. It was sitting on her dressing table and I checked to see if there was some left. There was a terrible pong from it and I quickly put the stopper in.

"What is the smell in here?" I asked pointing to the bottle.

"The woad colour is got from soaking the plant in urine and having it trampled on by trolls. That's the cause of the smell," Lodur explained.

Holding my nose, I turned back to face Cissy. "Listen, I've the Blue and here is the Indigo for you. You must take it and we'll go together. Call up the whirlwind and we'll head back to the school. We must do this before they all wake up," I said.

Cissy hesitated for a moment. "No, Bull. F is not a bad person, he wouldn't have done this to me. You go and I'll stay." She began texting in the code.

As before, a whirlwind started to form but then seemed to wrap itself in a knot. Two more times this happened and the whirlwind was soon tangled in three knots and wouldn't work. It clattered and whirred trying to untangle itself. The noise was sure to wake those in the hall.

"What's wrong?" I shouted.

"Freybensky is quite a wizard. He has wrapped the wind in three knots to stop you from leaving," Lodur said sadly.

"*Flaming Norah!* We're skewered," I said remembering the cook's fire where I'd still probably end up.

There was a long pause.

"No, we're not. I have my wish left and you can use that to take the colours, Bull," Cissy said.

"But you said you used it with the scorpion-men! You lied, Cissy! You could have saved Tricks." I was so angry the words rushed out. I wanted to pull at her hair but Lodur stopped me.

"I'm so sorry, Bull. I just wanted so much to get here. I wanted to hold onto my wish in case something ever happened to Freybensky. I really love him. It was going to be my wedding gift for him. I'm so sorry. I can't go back now." Cissy was sobbing as she made her wish. The whirlwind unravelled and wound about the room.

I was going to leave Cissy there, but I couldn't. No matter

what happened to Tricks I needed her to take the two colours back. I had decided to go on alone to the last colour.

"Yes, you can. No matter how much pain you have caused Cissy Hourihan, I can't leave you here. We've already lost Tricks and I'm not going to lose you as well." At the last moment I held out my hand to her. She looked surprised and hesitated for a moment before taking it and following me into the whirlwind.

Back at the Faery school, Cissy and I didn't speak much. Shimmer and the screech-owl watched as she took the goatskin of lazuli powder Blue and the bottle of woad Indigo from me and placed her hand on the spot. She typed in '**Raincolour**' with the last bit of battery time in my phone and was crying as the wall began to turn. We had swapped mobile phones as there was more battery time left in hers.

"I'll try and make it up to you and the others, Bull. I promise." Cissy looked at me.

"Sure," I said not really believing her. Nothing would bring Tricks back and she knew it. The TimeHole opened and Cissy, Blue and Indigo were gone.

20

THE COLOUR VIOLET

❋〰ℳ ℳ□●□◆□ ✝〉〈□●ℳ◆

Part 1. The Temple of Thoth

Freybensky was still out there and might come after me for helping Cissy escape. Not might, I thought, bound to like. I knew I needed to get as far away as possible and as quickly as possible. I texted Puffer.

'◈□〉〈■⅛ ℨ●□□■ℳ ⤳□□ ✝〉〈□●ℳ◆. ⅔□ ◆〉〈◆〰ℳ◆ ●ℳ⤳◆. ✝〰□ ⌖□ ✋ ●□□& ⤳□□ – ◈◆●●. Going alone for Violet. No wishes left. Who do I look for? – Bull.'

'✋○〰□◆ℳ□ – (Imhotep).' The answer came back. I showed it to Shimmer.

"That is a mood far back in time, Bull. The codeword you need is *"The Mummy's Tomb."* she said as she whispered something in the screech-owl's ear.

I typed it in FDTL and soon the whirlwind formed.

"Bye, Shimmer, see ya soon I hope," I whispered nervously.

"One moment, Bull."

"What is it, Shimmer?"

"I want the owl to go with you. He will be your guardian." She whistled softly and the owl flew over to sit on my shoulder.

"Thanks," I said gratefully as we stepped into the whirlwind.

The next thing I knew is that the owl and myself were in the middle of a very old building whose walls were covered with strange symbols. There were pictures of people who either looked like dog-headed apes sitting down or who had heads like birds with a long curved beak. There wasn't much light and every moving shadow caused by the flickering fire-torches in their holders on the walls made me more and more nervous.

From the shadows a tall man with long, silver hair and wearing what looked like a skirt came towards us. The owl screeched and flew off to sit on a high ledge where he could watch in safety.

"Who are you?" I asked.

"My name is Imhotep, he who comes in peace," he said in a weird voice. He had wrinkles like Puffer's, and they moved like ripples over his whole face as he smiled kindly at me. Sometimes the wrinkles made his face look like an ape and sometimes they would join together to make what looked like a beak. It was weird but no more weird than many of the things that had happened to us. "And you, my young friend, what are you and what do you want?" he asked.

"My name is Bull Sheehan," I answered and before I knew it I had started telling him the story of the quest. He waited until I was finished.

"What about you. Why is Violet or purple your colour?" He asked quietly.

"Because despite all the excitement I really just want peace and quiet," I answered. I wanted things the way they were.

"But the colour is very powerful. You must guard against living in your imagination." Imhotep sounded like my granny.

"At this moment, it's all I have like," I said grumpily.

"Well then, my brave young storyteller. You have come to the right place for your search!" he said, nodding his head.

"Why?" I asked, relieved.

"This is the Temple of Djehuti, whom some call Thoth and others Hermes, the three times great. Djehuti is the God of the

Moon, the lord of the hieroglyphs or 'Holy Words', the guardian of all storytellers and writers, and the keeper of Time. They are his roads that bring you from your world to ours. In this Temple are his magic books and the lists of the dead. It is here that you will find the fountain of all wisdom and knowledge, if you are worthy that is." Imhotep said this last part while looking deeply into my eyes.

"What do you mean?" I asked, wary of what he was getting at like.

"All knowledge may be used for good or evil, it is the wisdom to use that knowledge that is the gift of the Gods. I will need to know if you have been given the gift of that wisdom. Come with me?" He took me by the hand and led me through door after door of the building until we reached the last room. The owl screeched to halt as we got there and refused to follow us in.

In the centre of the room was a small black-coloured, pyramid-shaped, shiny rock over which hovered a large eye which was closed. Light was coming out from under the rock.

"Is this person, Bull, worthy, O great one?" Imhotep was on his knees and talking to the rock. Stone mad, I thought like.

Nothing happened for a moment but then the light seemed to get brighter around the rock. It began to glow a deep green colour. The eyelid started to flicker and suddenly it popped open. A beam of light shot out from the eye towards the wall, like when they're showing a film in a cinema. A whole lot of hieroglyphs, the picture-type symbols that the ancient Egyptians used for writing, appeared on the wall.

I looked at them, not having a clue like. There wasn't a whole lot of demand for learning how to read hieroglyphs in our school in Dripsey.

"What does it say?" I asked Imhotep.

"Watch!" he said as he waved his hand and the hieroglyphs changed into letters that I sort of recognised.

164

"Wicked!" I said, suddenly thinking of Tricks who would love to have seen it.

"*dd.t(w) n=f iw : m htp in wr(w) n ⟨bdw m dhwtt : m hb(w) nb '⟨ irrw n ⟨sir hnty-imntw ntr '⟨ n k⟨ n hry-sst⟨ kz mry m⟨'t*" The letters flickered on the wall as he read them out.

"I still haven't a clue like," I said.

"Translating into your language, it says, '*May 'Welcome in peace' be said to him by the great ones of Abydos at the Thoth-festival, and at all the festivals which are performed for Osiris-Khentyimentu, the great god, for the ka of the master of secrets, Bull beloved of Maat,*'" Imhotep translated. "In other words, Thoth the God thinks you are worthy of his help," he added with a smile.

"That's a relief. Who or what is *ka* and *Maat*?" I asked.

"*Ka* is your spirit, your courage, your loyalty and *Maat* is the goddess of Truth. The God is wishing you well in your search but is reminding you of the qualities you must have." Imhotep's face had wrinkled into an ape shape.

"May I ask the stone about the colour Violet?" I was looking at the green-glowing rock as I said this when suddenly four crossed lines appeared on the ground in front of us. "What's happening?" I asked.

"It is a game. You will have to play the God of the Moon for a part of its light, the colour that you seek is that part," Imhotep explained.

"What type of game?" I asked.

"We call it *eyes and ears* but I think in your world its known as 'noughts and crosses'. Do you know how to play?" he questioned.

Did I what! If you're someone like me who gets a bit bored in class at times, particularly with arithmetic like, then doodling and playing 'noughts and crosses' was the only way of getting through the class. Tricks and I were the best in the school. Old emerald-eye would be no match. "What do I do?" I asked enthusiastically.

"You are playing the *ear* and you can place it in any box just by thinking about it. It is a telepathic game." Imhotep spoke as he sat down on a nearby stool to watch. The game went on for what seemed like forever and every time I thought I had the stone fooled it figured out what I was up to. We had draw after draw after draw.

Suddenly I realised what was happening. The pyramid stone could read my thoughts and was anticipating my every move. I knew I would have to think of something else while I played. 'But what?' I wondered. Then it came to me. I remembered the frightening experience of kissing Suzy Tulips O'Farrell again, and thought of this in between making my moves.

A new game started. I was first to move this time and I teleplaced an *ear* in the bottom right box and then thought of Suzy. The stone glowed in confusion, wondering why my thought signals were so mixed-up like, and put an *eye* in the bottom middle box next to my ear. *(See the game at back of book.)*

'Oh! I've made a big mistake there,' I pretended to think, as I put an *ear* in the top middle box. The stone follows with an *eye* in the middle-middle box.

"I have you by the rocks now," I half shouted to the rock. "*Ear* in top right box. I've now two ways of winning and you can only block one."

The lines suddenly disappeared from the ground and for a second or so the pyramid stone glowed red with annoyance.

"You play well, my young storytelling friend and you have won your piece of light!" Imhotep, said with an impressed voice. "How did you do it? I've never been able to conquer the stone."

I was afraid to tell him my trick of thinking about Suzy so just said, "Luck, I suppose," and shrugged my shoulders.

"Look!" Imhotep pointed to the wall, which was flickering with new letters. "Thoth knows what's in your heart."

166

"What does it say?" I asked, a little worried after fooling it.

"In the Mysterious Tomb of the Queen Pharaoh from the seas lies the juice of the shells, the colour of the gods. That is the portion of my light that you seek. The owl will know the start, the book of the dead will know the end." Imhotep read the words as the eye closed shut and the letters vanished.

I was glad the stone was a good loser but I wished, more than ever, that Tricks was still around as I was dire at riddles. "Where's this Mysterious Tomb," I asked Imhotep, "and what does the stone mean by the colour of the Gods?"

"The Violet colour that you seek is also called shell purple because it is produced from special glands in the mouths of two shellfish found in the Middle Sea. The people who make this dye dive to the bottom of that sea and pull up all the shellfish and mix the juices from the two types. These shell fishermen are called the Phoenicians, or the purple people. They took so many shellfish for making the dye that the shellfish became very rare and the dye became very, very precious. It was even more precious than gold in fact, and is only used to colour the clothing of Pharaohs and Kings.

Many generations ago a young princess of the Phoenicians called Nefertiti, whose name means 'A beautiful woman has come', became the second wife of a Pharaoh in Egypt and as a wedding present brought with her the last pot of the purple-violet shellfish dye that her people had. The Pharaoh's only son was jealous of this princess who married his father and when his father died he caused her to be locked up alive in a tomb forever. The princess took all her belongings, including the pot of dye with her into the tomb where it has remained hidden ever since. Nobody has known where her tomb is but now, Thoth has pointed the way by telling you to go to the Mysterious Tomb." Imhotep's wrinkles changed into a long beak.

"Why is it called Mysterious?" I asked.

"Because the hieroglyphs in the tomb announce that the

mummy buried there is of a Pharaoh called Smenkhkare, who nobody knows anything about. There is very little in our history about this mysterious person," he said with a shrug of his wrinkles. "Some scholars think that Smenkhkare is actually Nefertiti."

"How do I get there?" I wanted to get going.

"You can walk. It's not far, perhaps half a morning. You must enter the Valley of the Kings and in the centre of the East Valley look for a tomb with the number KV55 written on it. When you go into the tomb, make your way to the end chamber. Here you must look for the hieroglyph '☜◉◉' carved on the wall and then move the magic brick on which the hieroglyph is found."

"Right! I'd better get going," I said without much enthusiasm. I didn't really fancy going there on my own like, particularly into mysterious tombs and things.

"I will come with you," Imhotep suddenly said.

"You will?" I asked, delighted.

"Sure. It is the wish of Thoth. The God thinks you'll be lost for words without my help." His wrinkles suddenly changed into a hat of ostrich feathers and I stood there gaping at him like. "We are in a desert and the sun is very hot. I need my shades," he said with a few minor adjustments to the wrinkles when he saw my puzzled look.

We'd just begun to walk out through the temple when a sudden thought came to me. "By the way. What would have happened if I'd lost the game of *eyes and ears*?" I asked very quietly.

"You would have become one of the pictures on the wall of the temple, one of the scribes for all eternity." He looked down at me and with a flick of his long hair smiled. "One of the dog-headed apes I think."

"Very funny!" I replied as we left the temple.

The bright sunlight made me sneeze like mad and when I

eventually stopped I had my first chance to take in some of the scenery. All around us was a fierce amount of activity and I could see hundreds of boats with triangular sails going up and down a nearby river and a long line of people winding their way along a narrow road into the mountains.

"What's going on?" I asked.

Imhotep looked around for a moment. His face and wrinkle-hat quivered as he spoke. "That is the river Nile and all those people walking into the mountains are part of the funeral procession for Meryatum, one of the sons of our great long-lived King, Osiris Usermaatre-setepenre or Rameses the Second. The tomb that they are taking him to for burial, is very near the tomb that we are looking for. We will have to be quick to get there first. They deal very harshly with tomb-raiders around here."

"What happens?" I asked, not really wanting to know, like.

"They stake you to the ground, cover you in honey and let the dung beetles eat you . . . slowly," he growled.

Enough said like, I thought as I followed him down the steps.

21

THE COLOUR VIOLET

✳〰️꟨ ꟽ◻●◻◆◻ ✞⟩◻●꟨◆

Part 2. The Mysterious Tomb

Imhotep decided to take a shortcut through the village of the workers who build and decorate the tombs. We followed the narrow path that took us up the side of the hill that overlooked the Valley of the King's graves and along the top of the ridge. Below us in the valley, all seemed quiet and the funeral procession was still a long way off. We were just about to start making our way down the hill when the telephone in my pocket bleeped. I took it out and saw there were five messages for me in the message-minder box. I opened the box and scrolled down.

*1: 'My greta Cissy, text me. I will come to get you – F'. I'd forgotten I had Cissy's phone and shook when I saw who sent the message. I scrolled down.

*2: 'School surrounded by tanks and girls from DSS. Be quick head, not much time-Atlas'. I scrolled again.

*3: 'F knows where you are – watch out – Puffer'.

*4: 'Travelling abroad? Keep in touch with Sky and Sea News – Queen Katie Allteeth-IL DOCE'. Things must be really bad at home, I thought, as I scrolled down to the last message.

*5: 'Skald – you will soon be a ghost writer – F'. The owl, who was sitting on my shoulder screeched when it saw that.

"Is everything as it should be?" Imhotep asked, concerned.

"Nothing is as it should be. We don't have much time?" I answered quietly.

We ran down the path as fast as we could and into the wide part of the valley near the tomb of the Pharaoh Seti I, which Imhotep told was the biggest and best in the valley. We crept close to the hillside so as not to alert the crocodile-headed guards standing near the nearby tomb that the funeral procession was heading for, until we found the entrance to the Mysterious Tomb. Somebody had written KV55 over the entrance and we dashed in before the crocodile guards saw us.

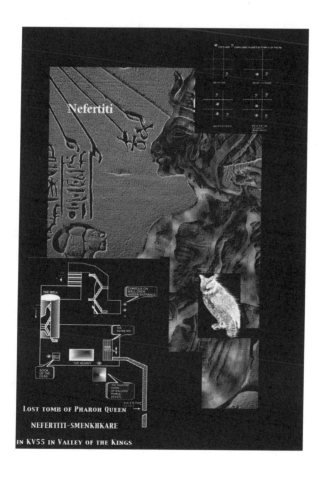

We had to walk down a very dark corridor until reaching a room at the very far end. Now the place was a mess like, with broken doors and part of the roof caved in. It was much smaller than I expected but there was a mummy's tomb in one corner with the lid half opened. When we looked in, the casket was empty.

"Tomb-raiders," Imhotep said without waiting for me to ask. "Look for the magic stone."

We searched everywhere for the stone without any luck and were just about to give up when the screech owl suddenly flew from my shoulder and towards one wall. By blending into the wall the owl looked out at us like one of the hieroglyphs.

"That is very clever," Imhotep said.

"Why?" I asked.

"The shape the owl is making is the sign for *em* or in, in your language. Your owl is pointing the way for you," he answered as he moved to the wall and started rubbing off the dust with his hand. By this stage his wrinkles had returned to the shape of a birds beak. "Look, here it is. Here is the magic stone."

I came up alongside him and could see '👁👁👁' carved into the rock. "Wicked," I whispered as I thought I heard a hissing sound behind me.

"Cover the eyes and the rock will open," Imhotep ordered.

I put my hands over the two eyes and suddenly a door in the wall opened. We had to go into a narrow passageway which first climbed a set of steps, went in a zig-zag fashion before going down a short flight of steps before reaching a large circular hole in the ground. I picked up a stone and threw it into the hole. After a long time I heard a splash, and then water sloshing about from its depths.

"It's a well and not a tomb," I groaned, fierce disappointed like.

"It is both a well and a tomb," Imhotep said.

"What do you mean?" I asked.

"The builders of this tomb connected it to the Nile river by underground pipes. In our world, every year the waters from the melting snows and rains of the Ethiopian Mountains flood the river and the land on either side. This is our sign of rebirth because it brings fertility to the country. When the Phoenician Pharaoh Queen, Nefertiti was put in the tomb, the rising water of the tomb would be a symbol of her rebirth every year," he explained.

"So what do we do?" I wondered.

"There should be a stairs in the well. We will climb down into the tomb." As Imhotep answered he was distracted by the hissing noise I'd heard earlier and looked back the way we'd come. "Quick!" He said urgently as he pushed me ahead of him.

There was a stairs and we climbed down and down for what seemed like forever. At the bottom there was water and as I stepped off the stairs it came up to my waist. The tomb was a large room and all the walls were painted with pictures of the princess and some of the things that happened in her life. She looked a bit like Shimmer only she had dark hair. I turned to Imhotep whose wrinkles were flapping about.

"What now?" I asked.

"Look for the Book of the Dead. It should be nearby," he said heading off into one corner. I followed him and we came to a pillar that held up the roof. On it were pictures and writing and Imhotep suddenly shouted. "This is it. This is the Book of the Dead. Now look for the ☻ sign. It will tell us where to go next."

We found the ☻ sign on one side and Imhotep read out what it said beside it – "*I Nefertiti lie in this tomb of imprisonment. My treasurers are hidden, to be shown only when the waters of rebirth arise,*" he read quietly.

"Let's look around like," I said and began to search the

room. We passed by a large black stone coffin, which had a carving on the lid in the blue lapis lazuli, I'd seen before, and gold of the same woman whose pictures were on the walls. There were other carvings of snakes and beetles and shellfish decorating the sides of the coffin. There was also hieroglyphic writing, which Imhotep read out.

"I am Nefertiti, beloved of Aten and the Pharaoh forever," he whispered. "That explains some of the mystery."

"Why?"

"Nefertiti had proclaimed herself Pharaoh and as she was buried alive she declared herself Pharaoh forever."

"Look over here!" I shouted pointing to a ? sign over what looked like a door in the wall beside the coffin. There were no handles and this time covering the eye sign did nothing.

"There must be a secret lever," Imhotep said. "Search again."

Directly in front of the coffin was another pillar on which marks were carved like lines. On one side was the pointing hand sign.

"What's that?" I asked pointing to the pillar.

"It's a Nilometer. It shows the level of the water as it rises with the flood. The ☜ sign shows the level it is at present," Imhotep answered.

"What did the book say? Something about the treasures being shown when the waters rise. What if we move the hand like?" I asked.

"Try it!" he agreed.

And I did. I was able to move the pointing hand sign up the pillar and as I did we could hear rushing water coming into the tomb.

Suddenly the coffin lid flew open and the mummy inside it sat up to look at us. At the same time the hole in the wall opened and when I looked inside there was lots of jewellery and pots. The water was nearly up to my neck when I finally saw a bottle of purple liquid.

"I have it. I have the Violet," I shouted as I stretched into grab it. The water was nearly at my mouth and I could hear the owl screeching behind me. "Push down the lever," I gurgled.

"Swim out!" Imhotep shouted.

Too late for that like. I had the bottle in my hand as the water went over my head. I started to pull it out but the door of the treasure room came slamming down. It caught my shirt. I tried holding my breath. I thought I saw Tricks smiling at me. I couldn't swim away. I blacked out.

I don't know how long later it was but all I remember was coughing and spluttering. The water had dropped again to my waist. The coffin lid of the mummy was closed but there was no sign of the owl or Imhotep. I called out for them. I couldn't move, my shirt was still trapped by the door.

I could hear a hissing sound. It was coming from the coffin. I looked across. One of the snake carvings had come alive and was squirming its way across the water towards me. I couldn't get away. I held onto the bottle of Violet. I screamed.

"Help. *Help!*"

Suddenly there was a whoosh and the owl came flying through the tomb and grabbed the snake. It landed on the coffin and was about to tear its head off when I heard the snake speak.

"Mercy. Please grant me mercy," it spat in a rasping hiss.

The owl looked at me and I held up my hand to stop it. Imhotep came back into the tomb.

"I'm sorry, my young friend. I couldn't save you as I cannot swim. I had to head to the stairs for safety after pressing down the lever. Are you . . ." He suddenly saw the owl holding the snake. ". . . that is a deadly viper snake and in our language is the symbol for the F sound of yours."

"I am **FFFFffffffffff**," the snake hissed.

"Why shouldn't I let the owl rip you apart?" I said.

"Because you are a good perssssssssson," it hissed.

175

I thought of Tricks and was about to let the owl get on with it like when I noticed the bottle of Violet glowing.

"You must use your wisdom to decide, my friend. Do you choose a good or evil path?" Imhotep asked.

I thought about it for a long time like but in the end I slowly shook my head. The owl let go of the snake and in a flash it turned into Freybensky the giant. He looked a bit brutal and there were huge scratch marks around his neck.

"I thank you, Skald, my brother, Puffer chose you well for your wisdom. In return I must now help you," he spoke as he started pushing the mummy's coffin to one side. I watched him carefully like, not trusting the F at all like. It took all his strength. "The crocodile guards are waiting at the tomb entrance for you to come out because I told them there were tomb-raiders in here and your phone won't work this far down. You will have to take the secret passageway out."

Freybensky was too big as a giant to go in, so he turned back into F the snake again and slithered into the passageway. Imhotep and me, with the owl sitting on my shoulder screeching at the snake every time he saw it, followed him down. We could hear the coffin moving back into position behind us and any light there was soon disappeared. We crawled and crawled in the darkness for ages; the owl, who had good sight and hearing in the dark, kept between me and F, in case he tried any fast moves, or shed his new skin like.

At last the tunnel came out into the sun and I was able to call up the whirlwind. Freybensky was himself again and I asked what happened after the wedding feast.

"When Skathanna and the Salmon Kings found I did not have a girl waiting for them there was an enormous fight. They wanted to take the *bifrost* Rainbow Bridge from our world in exchange. We won the battle but I lost many of my warriors."

"And Skathanna, what happened to her and the Salmon

Kings?" I asked knowing that they were responsible for stealing the colour from our world.

"Banished for a thousand lifetimes to a place they can cause no harm. Your world is safe for a long, long time," Freybensky said quietly, knowing that he would have no more excuses to go into chat rooms in our world.

"Right. I'm off so," I said as the whirlwind wrapped around me. Imhotep waved me goodbye and the next thing I knew Shimmer was running towards me with her hands held out.

I held out mine as well like, thinking she was going to hug me, but was sort of devastated when she reached for and took the owl from my shoulder. The owl winked back down at me before flying off and I laughed for the first time since Tricks drowned.

"I'll miss you, Bull Sheehan. People will talk about your journeys here in Faery World for ever," she said sweetly.

"Thank you for everything Shimmer and for lending me your owl . . . where's he gone anyway?" I asked.

"I'm right behind you." A voice that I recognised suddenly spoke. I turned to look.

"Lodur. It's you . . . you are the owl," I gasped with the shock of it like.

"Lodur is my husband," Shimmer said as she came and held his hand.

"You had better get going, Bull. Things are very bad in your world." Lodur spoke with a concerned frown. "We wish you the best of luck and hope that you are in time."

I typed in 'Raincolour' and the TimeHole opened up.

At the far side Puffer, Mister Penhaligan, Atlas, Jambo, Kegs and Cissy were waiting. They didn't seem as happy as I thought they would be, to see me and the Violet.

22

THE COLOUR OF RAIN

✳〰ℳ ☝□●□◆□ □↗ ☼☺)(■

The second I stepped through the map I knew I'd been away for a really long time as the need for food hit me with an almighty slap. I was so hungry like, I couldn't talk or move and I felt I was going to faint. Puffer immediately realized this and brought me over some bananas and chocolate, which I wolfed down. Atlas, Kegs, Cissy and Jambo were hovering near the window and would take turns looking outside before looking down at me. They all waited until I got my energy back and waited for me to speak first.

"How long have I been away?" I asked.

"Nearly a whole day," Jambo answered.

"What's happening?" I looked at the others hovering near the window.

"IL DOCE and Queen-to-be, Katie Allteeth are in town and have decided to make an example of the school. They are claiming it is the hideout for a group of dangerous, attention-seeking terrorists who threaten the New Kingdom of the Changing Environment, that they have established, with subversive colour bombs. At this very moment the Army and the DSS are surrounding the school with tanks and have given us one cower to come out otherwise they will flatten it." Mister Penhaligan spoke in a very serious and very frightened voice.

"The only attention-seeker I know is Sheevra Devine. She must have told them about our quest," I said angrily.

"It . . . it wasn't her, Bull, it was me," Kegs said quietly.

"What do you mean, Kegs?" I asked, puzzled like.

"Go easy on him, head, those multiple choice questions set by the Department of Changing Families are a torture than very few people can stand up to. They had the story of the quest bored out of him, before I could help him escape," Atlas answered for Kegs, as I went over and put my hands round his shoulders.

"Listen, dude, I understand. It's not your fault like. How is your Dad by the way?" I asked, trying to change the subject.

"In hospital with the PANDA virus. It's like somebody unplugged him, he's wasting away." Kegs had tears in his eyes.

"*Flaming Norah!*" I said, shocked like.

"Exactly," Kegs agreed with a shrug of his shoulders.

"That's not the worst of it, Bull," Cissy spoke quietly. I'd avoided eye contact with her as I doubted I would ever be able to forgive her.

"What do you mean?" I turned towards her.

"Your mum and sister are also in hospital," she said concerned, which was unusual for Cissy.

"Why?" I felt a sinking feeling in my stomach.

"SHAGDED disorder. They were watching the 'Changing Shades' programme together and started arguing over whether a black and white kitchen was better than a white and black one. Things got really out of hand and they were admitted to the psychiatric ward for evaluation," she said, not looking directly at me.

I said nothing for a long time, but looked around the classroom. Somehow I'd expected everything to be happy, having managed to recover all the colours like, but it wasn't like that. Everyone in the room was quiet, worried looking, afraid even. "There is one other problem." Puffer finally spoke. His wrinkles were nearly hitting his feet.

"What other problem could there be?" I asked.

"My plan to bring back the colour into the world was to transport all of the colours you have recovered to the volcano in Mount Etna in Sicily. It's erupting at the moment and you would need that type of intense heat to fuse them together, but, with the school surrounded we won't be able to get there," he said sadly, picking up the jar of Violet and looking at it. "And now they are going to flatten the school and us in it unless we come out. It is too late. We will have to surrender. I cannot bear the thought of having anything else happen to you, not after what my brother Freybensky tried to do. My guilt wrinkles could not stand it."

"He is an evil man, that F," Jambo said.

"Should be locked away," Kegs added.

"I'm so sorry," Puffer apologised.

"Not your fault, head. We can't choose our relatives." Atlas didn't seem too bothered and I took the opportunity to tell them about what happened in the tomb. When I finished Cissy was crying.

"I did love him," she whimpered.

"This is getting us nowhere. What are we to do?" Jambo asked.

None of us had a clue and we all slumped to the floor in silence. There was only 45 minutes left. Outside the school we could hear shouting from the girls in the DSS. They were having a great time like.

Suddenly there was a large, crashing noise followed by a brutal rumbling sound which got closer and closer. We all jumped up to look out the window, just in time to see a tank heading straight for us.

"*Flaming Norah!*" I shouted. "Scatter lads, it's coming straight in like."

We all rushed to hide behind Mister Penhaligan's desk at the far end of the room. The noise got louder and louder, there was a screeching sound and then the wall began to bulge beneath where the map was. The bulge got bigger and bigger until the barrel of a gun poked its way through the part of the map where Timbuktu was. The rest of the tank soon followed until it rolled to halt right in front of us. The room went quiet and we waited as the dust settled to see what was going to happen next.

"Let's get out of here, heads," Atlas whispered and we all started crawling towards the back door. The roof hatch of the tank opened. We froze.

"Where are you all going?" A very proper voice demanded. There was only one person who spoke like that.

"Sheevra!" We all shouted together, wondering what was going on in her hair extension of a head. She climbed up from the turret and then down to us in a coordinated general's uniform.

"I stole my mother's tank. I didn't agree with what they planned to do to you. Is there any way in which I might help," she announced, brushing some dust off her jacket.

"Miss Devine. Are there 'starburst' rockets in that tank?" Puffer asked suddenly.

"Yes, I think so. My mother uses them instead of fireworks," she said.

"Good. I have an idea." Puffer's wrinkles were dancing. "Mister Malone and Mister Kitangiri, climb up into the tank and bring out a 'stardust' shell. Mister Sheehan and Mister Murphy, I want you to bring back an ordinary shell. Miss Hourihan, go with my nephew into his office and get all the colours ready."

"What are we going to do?" I asked him.

"I will explain in a few moments. Go ahead and I will catch up with you. I want to have a private word with Miss Devine." Puffer shooed us away.

Atlas and Jambo brought the 'starburst' shell and Kegs and I brought the ordinary one back into the office. They were fierce heavy like but we were afraid if we dropped them they would explode. We were sweating when Puffer came into the office carrying a large roll of tinfoil and two spoons. Mister Penhaligan and Puffer straight away began unscrewing the pointed titanium tips of the shells. When they had them off Puffer looked at us.

"The 'starburst' shells are like huge fireworks and are used to light up a battlefield at night. They generate tremendous heat, more than enough for our purposes, I think," he said with some seriously satisfied wrinkles as he pulled out his orb-watch to check on the time. "We only have fifteen minutes."

"What do you want us to do?" Cissy asked.

"I want you to start cutting the tin foil into small pieces."

"What about us, head?" Atlas asked.

"You and Mister Kitangiri spoon out about a quarter of the firework powder in the 'starburst' shell and Mister Sheehan and Mister Murphy, you do the same with the ordinary shell." He watched as we did this, looking anxiously at his watch. When we had enough removed he nodded.

"Right, into the space you've made in the 'starburst' shell I am going to put in the colours. Like this!" Puffer shouted with excitement.

He first poured in some of the Violet shellfish dye of Nefertiti and this was followed by the Indigo woad of Freybensky, the Blue lazuli powder of JinkJinn, the Green coral of MacUbartutu, the Yellow tibar of Timbuktu, the Orange of the Golem, and finally the Red concoction of Bolus Mendez. Once finished he screwed the tip of the shell back on.

"What about the other shell?" Jambo asked.

"Miss Hourihan I want you to pack the space we've made in that shell with as much of the tin foil as you can manage." He watched as she did this and as Mister Penhaligan screwed the tip back on had a quick look at his orb-watch again.

"We have five minutes. Get into the tank Miss Devine.

182

Mister Malone and Mister Kitangiri will load the shell packed with tin foil. I want you to fire it as high as possible into the sky over the town. When that's done I want you to load the 'starburst' shell and wait for my signal. Understood!" We nodded. "Good. Get moving and . . ." We waited for his wrinkles to settle a bit. ". . . good luck. We only have one chance at this."

Sheevra Devine paraded her way to the tank and after waiting for us to load the shells and get in, started to turn the turret so that the gun would face the town. I think she forgot where she was like, because as the gun turned it whipped off half the roof of the school like a knife through butter. All of the Army and DSS girls were cheering wildly but dropped to the ground when Sheevra pressed the trigger and the gun suddenly fired the first shell over their heads.

It soared up and up and up above the clouds, so high up it started falling again. Suddenly it exploded and the tin foil was scattered everywhere and you could see the pieces floating down to land on the clouds. Those same clouds started getting dark and after a few rumbles rain began to fall in torrents towards the ground.

I then knew what Puffer had done. In very dry parts of the world the scientists called this sowing seeds of tin foil in clouds to make rain.

As the first raindrops came in through the gap in the roof Puffer shouted. "Now, Miss Devine. Fire the 'starburst' shell *now*!" He got me to bang on the side of the tank. Almost immediately the gun fired again and this time we watched as the shell flew out over the town and up into the middle of the rain. Suddenly it exploded and there was a massive burst of light in the sky that even brightened the shadows under the eyes of some of the DSS girls.

We waited and waited and waited but nothing else happened. The sparks of light fizzled out and we just stood there in the rain looking up.

We had failed.

The Army and DSS girls rushed towards the school and surrounded us. They made a big show of hassling us as IL DOCE and Queen-to-be Katie Allteeth arrived at the school. They lined us all up against the wall and started filling in application forms for the Happy Gulag detention centre. I could see that Kegs was beginning to crack. He couldn't take any more questions like. Sheevra was hauled out of the tank and had her uniform and hair extensions confiscated by IL DOCE. Atlas's pockets were searched and a tin of funny-looking leaves were found and taken away for examination. Jambo looked like he was going to start stuttering again and Cissy was worried about her snakes.

They were bundling us into a truck to take us to the Happy Gulag when the rain finally eased off and stopped.

"*Look!* Look up there!" Mister Penhaligan shouted as he pointed to the sky above us.

STARBURST SHELL AND THE RAINBOW

"The Colour of Rain!" Puffer said with fluttering wrinkles.

"It's . . . it's a . . . rainbow. I can see a rainbow," Katie Allteeth spoke for everyone. "I can see colours, sweetie." She turned to IL DOCE, whose face drained of all the colour he never had.

It took a while for the eyes of the Army and DSS girls to adjust and to fire up the parts that detect colour but soon everyone was chasing around shouting, 'Colour is back, Colour is back'. They then quickly realised the horrible colour combination of uniforms they were wearing and rushed off home to change.

IL DOCE tried to stop them but they ignored him. After all he was wearing a jacket with purple and orange stripes and green trousers. Even Katie Allteeth began to see him in a new light and after throwing her tiara at him jumped into Missus Devine's tank and drove off at speed into a sunset that had not been seen for a long time.

23

THE CROCK OF GOLD

✳︎〰︎♏︎ ♏︎♑︎ ♑︎⬜︎⬜︎♏︎♑︎♑︎ ⬜︎♑︎ ♑︎♑︎⬜︎●︎♎︎

We were wandering around the schoolhouse looking at all the damage and wondering what we were going to do about it. Everyone was a bit caught up in their own thoughts and didn't notice IL DOCE sneaking away, his crown between his legs and a shadow of his former self.

My dad had rushed up to the school to see if I was all right before heading off to collect my mum and sister from the hospital. Apparently everybody in the hospital wanted to go home for a change of clothes.

Atlas was carefully folding up what was left of the map, saying he wanted to hold onto it. Mister Penhaligan told him he could. I couldn't feel happy about what we'd managed to do. Something was missing. Puffer saw me kicking out at the wall and came over. He pulled out his orb-watch to look at it.

"My work here is almost done, Mister Sheehan. It is time for me to go." He put his hand on my shoulder. "You should be very proud of what you have done."

"I wish I was . . . but," I mumbled.

"Look outside." Mister Penhaligan pointed to where the window once was.

I lifted my head slowly.

"*Flaming Norah!*" I screamed. Everyone turned to look as

well. It was a wicked moment like. Who did we see walking up the road, whistling and knocking off the heads of yellow dandelions with a stick, only Tricks Kirby. It was really weird like.

T
R
I
C
K
S

C
O
M
E
S

H
O
M
E

"*Wicked*. (Scream this out at the top of your voice, if you like.) Go on you good thing!" We all shouted together as we ran towards the hole in the wall to go and meet him. He was waving at us.

I suddenly saw that Sheevra Devine held back. She looked like she had lost something else and I stopped as well. I don't know why like. I just did.

I looked at Sheevra, who had small tears on her cheek and then at Mister Penhaligan, who also looked like he was about to cry. I was really puzzled.

"How Sir? How did Tricks get back?" I asked.

"Sheevra had never used her wish. Puffer reminded her about it before we started packing the shells. She used it for him." Mister Penhaligan's face was twisting up. He started snuffling and looking for his hanky. "Excuse me for a moment, Bull I want to get something from what's left of my office." He left quickly. I bet you he was crying as well like.

I turned round to look for Puffer but he too had vanished. Sheevra and I were in the classroom alone, looking out at Atlas, Jambo, Kegs and Tricks dancing in a circle on the road. Cissy was standing back a bit, afraid of one of the others telling her to get lost, but then Tricks grabbed her hand and pulled her into the circle. We stood there watching them. I didn't know what to say like but then Sheevra looked over at me and smiled, not a hair out of place, and suddenly there was a really warm feeling across my chest, like after the ointment my Mum rubs when I have a cold like.

I don't know what came over me but I grabbed her and kissed her. Now it wasn't a big lip kiss, mind, just a little one on the cheek like. There was a taste of salt and vinegar crisps and I pulled back as quick as I could. The lads had said that if you give a girl a big lip kiss then you had to be really, really nice to them for ever more. Buy them presents and stuff and do the things they want to do. Nah! I was too cute for that like.

I thought like!

The problem was (Whisper this – my instructions as I don't want the other lads to hear.) that Sheevra Devine suddenly kissed me back and after that everything changed again.

But then, that's another story like!

See ya! May the colour be with you.

Bull Sheehan signing off.

Appendices

Conversion of writing to Faery Dimension Texting Language.

Capitals	FDTL Capitals	Small letters	FDTL small
A		a	
B		b	
C		c	
D		d	
E		e	
F		f	
G		g	
H		h	
I		i	
J		j	
K		k	
L		l	
M		m	
N		n	
O		o	
P		p	
Q		q	
R		r	
S		s	
T		t	
U		u	
V		v	
W		w	
X		x	
Y		y	
Z		z	

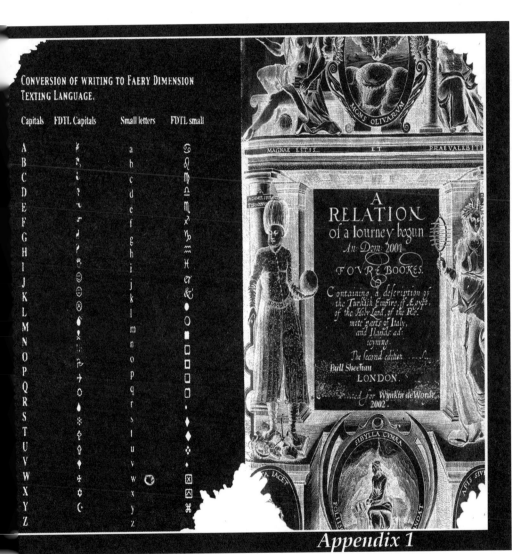

A
RELATION
of a Iourney begun
An: Dom: 2001
FOVRE BOOKES.

Containing a description of
the Turkish Empire, of Ægypt,
of the Holy Land, of the Remote parts of Italy,
and Ilands ad-
icyning.

The second edition
Bull Sheehan
LONDON.

Printed for Wynkyn de Worde,
2002.

Appendix 1

Sixteen ingredients for making the colour Red:

(Made in combinations of four)

1. **Mercury** (Quicksilver)
2. **Copper.**
3. **Essence of Kermes resin.** (From insects)
4. **Iron.**
5. **Red lead.**
6. **Sulphur.** (Mount Etna or other volcano)
7. **Tin.** (From Tintagel in Cornwall; Puffers place.)
8. **Dragons blood.** (Got when an elephant sits on a dragon)
9. **Vinegar.**
10. **Fresh Juice of Turnsole.** (A plant that follows the sun.)
11. **Root of *brazil* tree.** (*Caesalpinia braziliensis* or *crista*)
12. **Madder.** (Another plant)
13. **Crushed Cochinal Crusts.** (More insects)
14. **Oil of Lily's.**
15. **Crystal of Sand.** (Glass from Venice)
16. **Sweat from Pigs Back** (Not a pet one, they don't sweat)

THE MAGIC SQUARE

16	3	2	13	=	34
5	10	11	8	=	34
9	6	7	12	=	34
4	15	14	1	=	34
=	=	=	=		
34	34	34	34		

Work out how many combinations of four numbers gives you 34.
(Clue: 8 straight lines; 1 of middle numbers, 2nd numbers, 3rd numbers, opposites; 4 corners; 2 diagonals etc.)

Appendix 2

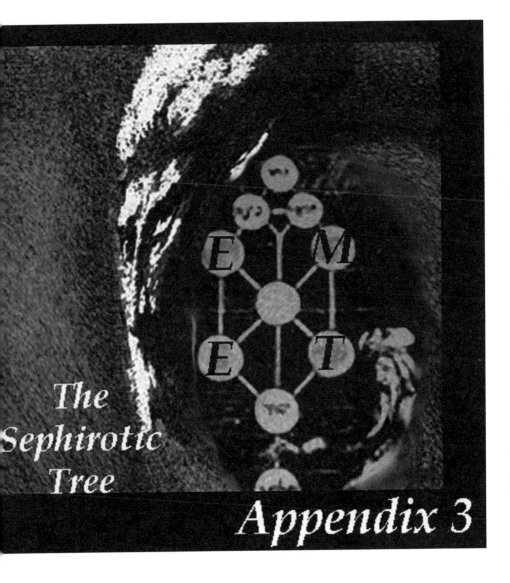

The
Sephirotic
Tree

Appendix 3

THE ROCKS

LEO

VIRGO

LIBRA

SCORPIUS

SAGITTARIUS

Appendix 4

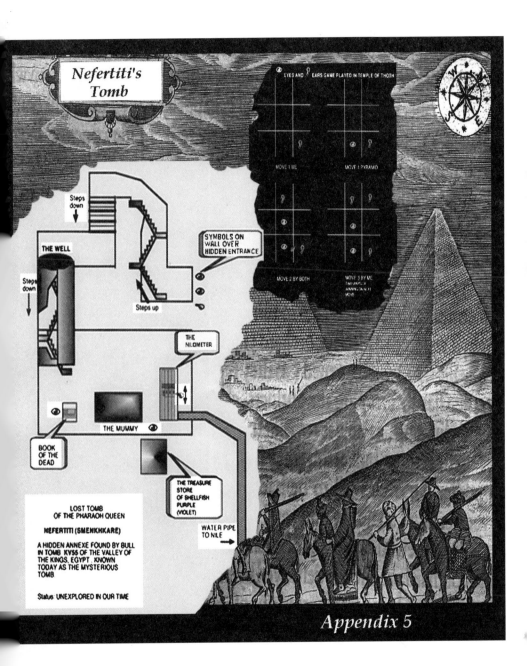

Nefertiti's Tomb

EYES AND § EARS GAME PLAYED IN TEMPLE OF THOTH

MOVE 1 ME   MOVE 1 PYRAMID

MOVE 2 BY BOTH   MOVE 3 BY ME

Steps down

THE WELL

Steps down

Steps up

SYMBOLS ON WALL OVER HIDDEN ENTRANCE

THE NILOMETER

THE MUMMY

BOOK OF THE DEAD

THE TREASURE STORE OF SHELLFISH PURPLE (VIOLET)

WATER PIPE TO NILE

LOST TOMB OF THE PHARAOH QUEEN

NEFERTITI (SMENKHKARE)

A HIDDEN ANNEXE FOUND BY BULL IN TOMB KV55 OF THE VALLEY OF THE KINGS, EGYPT. KNOWN TODAY AS THE MYSTERIOUS TOMB.

Status: UNEXPLORED IN OUR TIME

Appendix 5